A
Series
of
Events

Steve Crapo

ISBN: 1466245247
ISBN-13: 9781466245242

A Quartet of Riffs

We are more resilient than we give ourselves credit for, and life is a naturally carrying forward process, we just don't know where it's taking us.

-Carson Arrowsmith

"You say your clinic is called Simone deB, and I assume you mean Simone de Beauvoir. Do you want to be like her?"

"Well, if you mean divesting myself of bourgeois respectability, I'm not even close on that one. But as I told you a minute ago, I want to be the one who invents who I am."

-Morgan Alar answers the question

Madness sucks the humanness from a person. There are things people should not do to each other and madness opens the door to doing those things.
-Carson Arrowsmith

I've lived a privileged life and I have to leave it behind. For me life was always out there, beckoning to me, and there was a plan: become a doctor, practice medicine, achieve status in the community, have a relationship with a man. In short, I could have what I want. What has happened is that lived life has trumped the planned life, the expected life. I can't put life behind me. There will always be obstacles, surprises, roadblocks, and especially detours that will throw me off the grid. It's the life my patients struggle with, why shouldn't I?
-Morgan Alar

Prologue

It is possible that Viktor Perdu had been a part of Morgan's life for some time before she met him face to face. Yet, she is now convinced that it was this first meeting that set off the series of events that disassembled her life for the next several months, a disassembling that was both painful and frightening, and that its effect on her would continue beyond the actual events and reverberate past her own life, reaching into the lives of her friends as well. There were other incidents, albeit vague and diffuse, that could have been the initial attack. There was the possibility that he had been at Au Courage the evening she met Omar Rome. Then there was the break-in at her studio. However, Morgan always returns to that initial meeting at Café Simone deB where he played the role of a patient.

Her initial image of him is still etched in her memory.

He was in autumn colors–brown corduroy pants, brown tweed jacket, and a beige sweater over a yellow oxford shirt–all oversized and generously cut. Hunched forward with a leg crossed over the middle of the other, and his jacket in his lap there was the impression of an elegant pile of wool and tweed cloth fouled by dank, spent tobacco smoke. His hair was blond, parted in the middle, and falling straight to his shoulders where it curled up ever so slightly. The pale skin of his face emphasized its delicate features (His eyes were a dark, mysterious color of brown.), especially his thin, sensual lips.

The entire session had been disjointed with her fighting for control. His entrance had created the stage for the dissonance.

Leading the way, Viktor strode confidently down the hallway and into her consultation room. With the same familiarity he immediately went to the far end of the sofa, sitting with his back wedged in the corner. It was as if it were his tenth or twentieth session, or that he was familiar with the plan of the room.

He foiled her attempt to start the session by reaching up and switching off the lamp on the small table at the end of the sofa. Other lights still illuminated the office, but Viktor was cast in a soft shadow.

"OK?"

"Yes. OK."

Morgan remembers that she then watched as Viktor slipped his hand into the inside pocket of his jacket, extracting a pouch of tobacco and a packet of cigarette paper. She watched as he carefully rolled a cigarette with slender nicotine stained fingers. Then, after removing a box of matches from the coat pocket, he searched the room, a quizzical look on his face.

"Ashtray. There are no ashtrays in this room."

"The entire building is a no smok-ing area."

Viktor sighs, continuing to hold cigarette and matches. "Pity. Always struggling with rejection, and have it directed at me not five minutes into my session by my therapist."

"Is this the issue? Is it rejec-tion we need to talk about?"

"Thanks for seeing me so late. Are we alone?"

"No. My partner Carson Arrowsmith is here."

"Ah! Always good to have a man around." Viktor removes a match from its box.

"Getting started is not always easy. Perhaps…."

"Is your father living?"

This interchange set the stage for the rest of their conversation. She would ask a question or offer a possible opening for discussion and Viktor would respond with a question requesting personal information from her or offer a statement that seemed unrelated to anything that had been said earlier.

In this surreal atmosphere, rendered interpersonally chaotic by Viktor's strange autism, Morgan felt disjointed and off guard.

"Fathers are important. My father, before he died, deserted my mother and me. He left for work one day and never returned. I think he did not like us—he wanted a better family. We had lost favor. Out there somewhere was one he could favor. I think it killed my mother. She died of a heart attack soon after."

Three quarters of the way through the hour Viktor had nonchalantly reached over and turned the clock on the table around so that Morgan could no longer see the time. Before Morgan could respond…

"You haven't shared…" (He makes a point to stress *shared* by drawing it out.) "…Whether your father is living or not."

"He's dead."

"Pity. How?"

"Hiking accident; in the Sierras."

Finally, Morgan had to check the time by using her watch. Viktor had smiled…

"Are you planning to say, our time is up, doctor?"

Stammering like a rookie therapist, Morgan fell into the trap, saying that it was.

Leaving the office for the waiting room, Viktor had delivered his last mind-numbing blow…

"Alas, my poor father was also lost in a hiking accident. I think it was somewhere in Europe."

In the waiting room Morgan had tried to schedule their next meeting during regular hours, but Viktor had resisted. Morgan had finally agreed to another late evening meeting.

"Nine o'clock then. I'll see you at this time next week."

Perdu had smiled. "Yes, you will see me again."

Morgan stood in silence, waiting for the sound of the door to the street opening and closing. Before she heard those sounds, the sweet smell of tobacco drifted around her.

It took a week to find out that she would see him only that one time. Viktor did not come to the second meeting.

Morgan did not talk to anyone, not even Carson, about her strange encounter with Viktor Perdu, convincing herself that he was psychotic and she would never know why he had made the appointment. She had been reduced to a hapless bystander as he had struggled, by himself, with his internalized demons.

Still, she remained disturbed by the encounter—*creeped* out, as her younger patients would say. Most disturbing was his constant gazing at her. He would raise his cigarette almost to his lips, and then drop his hand back into his lap and smile-a shy embarrassed smile-while his eyes traveled over her body from head to toe. It did not seem sexual to Morgan. Rather (She came to this later), it seemed that he was trying to memorize her so he could suck her into his schizophrenic world making her one of his delusional objects.

Chapter One

Eros Carouses

Paris is muggy, its sky obscured by a canopy of gray clouds. The warm stickiness will continue to cling to both Parisian and traveler alike until the leaden clouds give up their rain.

Carson Arrowsmith detaches himself from the swirling boulevard crowd and ducks into *Les Deux Magots* snagging what may be the last empty table. Around him cafe life is in full swing. People with their green chairs pulled close to small round marble topped green iron tables cluttered with glasses of beer or wine, or a *café* or *thé*, bottles of champagne on ice, salads, *assiettes*, a *croque monsieur* form small universes dedicated to the ages old pleasure of eating, drinking and talking together. He orders a *demi*.

To his right is *Saint Germain des Prés*. Opening out onto the Place is rue Bonaparte. *Cafe Bonaparte*, claiming the corner of the Place-where *Appolinaire* ends-is, like *Les Deux Magots*...overflowing.

Leaving his duffels in his room at *Les Degrés de Notre Dame*, he had hoisted his backpack and headed for *Place Maubert* and then *Boulevard Saint Germain*, happy to be back in Paris.

Carson looks out at the busy boulevard awash with people hurrying here and there, some stopping to greet each other, mothers with infants, students, tourists, while others meet and slip under the awning to settle at a table. His iPhone vibrates against his leg. It's the text message from Jon Cade that he has been waiting for-the combination to the entrance of the building where Jon and his wife, Leda, are renting an apartment.

Carson finishes his beer and, after settling *l'addition* with the waiter, retrieves his backpack from the back of his chair and leaves the sanctuary of the *terrace*.

After buying an umbrella from *Monoprix*, and several bottles of *vin du pays* from the wine store in the Shell Station on Boulevard Raspail Carson arrives at Jon and Leda Cade's apartment building. Using the combination Jon sent him, he ducks through the small wooden door, a small portal cut into the massive wooden gate protecting the courtyard from the outer world, and follows the cobblestones to the entrance of the apartments. He pushes the button next to *Dupre*, the couple renting to the Cades.

"*Allô?*"

"It's Carson Arrowsmith. I'm here for dinner with the Cades."

The woman's voice is definitely American. "Third floor, top of the stairs."

There is a buzzing and Carson lets himself in.

By the time he has climbed the worn stone stairs, covered in the center by a rug held in place by brass rods, his eyes have adjusted to the subdued light. Reaching the landing of the third floor, the silhouette back-lighted by the open door of the apartment has become a woman. Tall and slender, she is wearing blue jeans with black leather flats and a rose-colored cotton sweater. The sleeves are pushed above her elbows. Under the V-neck of the sweater there is the scoop of a black T-shirt calling attention to the swelling of her bosom.

There is a striking similarity between her face and that of *Modigliani's Woman on a Cushion*. It is the subtle complexity of emotions and beauty created by Modigliani's brush strokes that he sees in the real woman. With a catch of his breath he recalls the nude's body reclining on the cushion, and wonders about the real woman's body.

"Carson?"

"Yes."

"Hi. I'm Morgan Alar."

They shake hands–hers is soft, he would like to hold it longer–and Carson follows her into the apartment where the aroma of fresh vegetables, olives, and anchovy fill the room. Her eyes, very clear, are green. Carson estimates that she is in her early to mid forties.

Morgan performs her own assessment. He has a nice smile. He looks to be in his late thirties, early forties; there is no wedding ring. His hair, short and stylishly cut is light brown. Small black-rimmed glasses give him the look of an academic. Closer inspection reveals several small surgical scars. Basal cells removed? Battle scars? A romantic Morgan favors the latter. With his complexion, there will be more damage in the future. Still, he is cute.

Morgan takes the bottles of wine from him, peering into the bag. "Ah! Rosé. Let's put them in the fridge. Leda and Jon, and I suppose Martin, are out shopping for the main part of the dinner.

I have been left here to do the pizza. Want to help?"

Her skin is creamy bronze-like a rich tan-but more likely hints at an interesting cultural blending. "I sure do." He sees a glass of white wine on a wooden table in the center of the kitchen. "Not too early for some wine…."

"Not at all." Grabbing a glass from a cupboard next to the refrigerator Morgan pulls a bottle of white wine from the refrigerator and pours him a glass. "There."

"I've got to get this dough made so it will have enough time to rise." She has moved to a wooden table in the center of the small kitchen where there is a food processor, flour, yeast and salt on the counter surrounding a jar of olive oil. "You can pit and chop those olives-need about half a cup-and then slice the onions. OK?"

Carson sees the olives and the onions by the sink. "I'll get right to it."

The processor begins to rumble at slow speed. "You're the psychologist."

"Yes.   You're the psychiatrist."

"Yes. How far back to you go with Jon?"

"Two years, maybe, not more."

"How'd you meet him?"

Carson remembers the incident clearly. "We were both in the Bay Area; he was on some business and I was up to see a friend.

"It was late-nine-thirty, ten-and each of us was waiting at an intersection for the light to change."

He remembers Shattuck and University, a McDonalds on one of the corners. The street had a sheen of water from the rain and it reflected into the night, mixing with car lights, street lights and the glow coming from the businesses that were still open to create a scene that was more light and motion than detail.

"This blind guy was trying to cross the street and had lost his direction. He had bumped into several of the stopped cars and was heading into the intersection.

"The young man had a cane but after hitting a car with it and then bumping another, the combination of disorientation and worry cancelled out his fragile means of finding his way. Looking around, I realized that every one was watching without doing anything, and that the guy was heading into the center of the intersection.

"Both Cade and I jumped from our cars at the same time, retrieved him and helped him get across the street. The light had changed and we had to get back to our cars, so we nodded to each other and moved on." Carson remembers that a guy on a motorcycle had yelled, Way to go, dudes, at them.

Carson has finished his chopping; the olives are in a bowl, the onions piled on a wooden cutting board. Morgan is finished with the dough, puts it in a bowl with plastic wrap over it, and places it on the shelf beneath the wooden table.

"The next day we saw each other at a pizza place and had lunch together. We laughed about leaving our cars with engines running and commiserated about how no one did anything–being satisfied to be spectators. We've stayed in contact ever since. He's a nice guy. How'd you meet him?"

"Wound up rather tight. I met him when I spent a year at the University of Washington. He knew my father. Since then Leda and I have become very good friends. Actually we're now long distance friends; we e-mail and Skype. It was Jon who invited me to spend some time with them here in Paris."

"Sounds like we both have long distance relationships with Jon and Leda."

"That's true. Actually though it's Jon, Leda, Martin and me at the present." As an afterthought she adds, "Well, maybe you now…."

Her teeth are white against the bronze of her skin. The subtle lighting of the kitchen gives her face a reflective radiance that is emphasized by the silver and brass rings dangling from her ears. There is a small white scar across the bridge of her nose and another shows faintly just above her lip, on the left side. Her vivacity and eagerness is very appealing.

Morgan goes to the tiny dishwasher that is in the alcove that was home to a water heater before the kitchen was modernized and pulls down the door. She is surprised at the lack of awkwardness between them. She has felt comfortable with Carson from the start.

"Here. Help me put these things on the table."

After a couple of trips to the table and back they stop in front of the almost empty washer. "I wish Jon wasn't so stiff. Sometimes he acts like a stuffed shirt. I think he's a very complex guy, but he never shows it."

She goes to the refrigerator, and retrieving the bottle of white wine from it, fills their glasses. There is a pause in the activity and their conversation as they each take a sip of a cold, dry wine of Provence. As Morgan takes a sip, she peers at him over her glass.

Carson thinks she is trying to see within him, looking for a quality, or hint of a sensitivity, that will clear the way for a new path of conversation. Apparently she has found what she is looking for; she resumes talking about Jon.

"It seems more pronounced these days, especially between him and Leda. They have become so tense around each other, and when they aren't carping there are the sly digs."

"Doesn't sound good."

"Martin has become more of a fixture. I'm not saying there is something going on between he and Leda, but you should see how she lights up when he is around. I think she wants something from Jon that she is not getting, and she is drawn to Martin because it is there with him. I know she wants whatever it is from Cade but he seems oblivious and she is looking to Martin…." Her voice trails off, and then, "This is dangerous, I know. It's become more serious, too.

"I know the plan was for Leda and Jon to meet you here, spend a week before going to Nice and then back to the States. But for some reason–well the reason is obvious–she invited Martin.   When Jon found out, he invited me."

Morgan removes some more dishes from the washer, taking them to the table; Carson follows suit, trailing behind her into the small dining room.

"That's why you're not here, Martin is at the Madison, and I'm on the couch in the drawing room."

"I had no idea…."

"I don't expect you to do anything.   It does feel good to talk about it, but I guess we're bystanders in this.   I suppose it will play itself out while we watch.   I wish Martin wasn't so eager to join the mix."

"I'm very fond of Jon.   I know he's an intellectual and he likes routine, but we do have good conversations.   We are long distance friends, though…maybe he'll bring something up and we'll be able to talk. Maybe we'll get to know each other better in the next week. I don't know Leda very well."

"That's why I came even though I knew too well I was a pawn in their marital warfare. You know, change the chemistry."

"Right. Maybe we can tip the balance."

For an instant she scrutinizes him, apparently again wrestling with some internal quandary. Carson imagines that her external and internal realities have lost their balance, and she is trying for realignment.

He smiles at her. Perhaps she's having the same reaction he did when he saw her for the first time. Contagious? He hopes so.

Cute. Interesting. *Ah!* This puts her on the verge. She knows this can become something. She imagines letting herself tumble into free fall, though she knows it will not carry her forward. She feels a tingling on the back of her legs–excitement tinged with apprehension.

"You going to Aix with Jon and Leda?"

"Right. Then Nice. I thought it would be fun to spend a couple of days in Paris before going there. You?"

"I'm going to Geneva tomorrow to meet two friends. Blanca is the daughter of my mentor Bernie Lane. She has a best friend, Ari. Bernie is footing their bill. From Geneva the three of us are going to Greece."

"Where are you returning to in the States?"

Morgan hesitates, feeling uncertain about how much information to reveal to Carson. Then: *Why not?* "I want to start my psychotherapy practice. Bernie wants me to work with him–he has a nice suite of offices in Berkeley. I think he hopes Ari and Blanca can sway me to settle in Berkeley. I do like Seattle, though, and I have a nice apartment there. Anyway, I'm hoping the pieces will fall into place during this trip."

Carson has noticed Morgan's hesitation, but decides to ignore it. "Well for what it's worth, my plans are to start a practice in Berkeley when I get back."

Morgan fills their glasses.

"I met my ex in Paris. Ex boyfriend, that is." Morgan smiles and slips her hand beneath the neck of her sweater and adjusts her strap. She repeats herself. "Ex boyfriend…history, now. You?"

"If you mean ex, no, no ex."

"Got a girl back home?"

Does she like to cuddle? "No. I just finished my post-doc. I had a lot of friends to hang out with but not a girl-friend. You?"

"I dated a guy for a while in Seattle, but he turned out to be a lizard. It didn't work out."

"Lizard?"

"Everything by the numbers." As soon as the words leave her mouth it sounds too personal a disclosure; she hopes Carson won't comment.

Carson wonders if she's telling him there may be a reason beyond the pro-fessional for returning to Seattle-still a tug…unfinished business, but quickly rules it out—he's sure Morgan does not hang out with lizards.

Morgan is relieved that Carson just shrugs. "So. Here we are, in our forties, I am anyway, and a serious relationship doesn't seem to be on the horizon.

"Not even the tiniest of blips on the radar. Marriage seems something to avoid. I don't think I'm ready for something…you know…I like being single."

"Me, too. Although when I was playing ball what I wanted was to get to the Bigs, marry, and have children."

"Playing ball?"

"Baseball. I was pretty good until I wrecked my shoulder during a double play at second."

"Jeeze, Carson…that's not good. Couldn't be repaired?"

"No. But, you know, it turned out for the best—I like where I'm at now."

Morgan is leaning against the sink. "Welcome to modernity."

Carson pulls on his ear. "I guess so. "I wonder. I don't think I'm on board yet."

Morgan smiles. Then, as she did earlier, she stares. Carson imagines she is making some kind of decision that involves him, but is her choice alone to make.

He likes her. Morgan is easy to talk to. In a short time a familiarity has grown between them, and some of her actions now seem to be imbued with a sense of intimacy, or at least familiarity. He thinks they are both guilty of indulging in some bravado. Something like, I'm single, no attachments; and I'm not looking for anything serious. He guesses it's serious, but kind of silly given the frisson he feels oscillating between them.

She closes the dishwasher door. "I don't think there's anything else we can do. Leda wants to set the table."

They hear the clatter of steps on the stairs, and then the key in the lock. On the way to the door Morgan and Carson reach the kitchen doorway at the same time and hesitate. For an instant, they are close, gazing into each other's eyes. Morgan can feel the heat of his body; Carson feels the boundaries between them soften and blur.   Then they are in the hallway greeting Jon.

Jon Cade is feeling sorry for himself, and he is use to feeling that way.   He also knows that if he can somehow let Leda in on his feelings, it will soften her attitude toward him.   Still-there is a sense of unease he does not understand. His nerves are on edge; it's the kind of nervousness that comes with the antici-pation that something upsetting is about to happen.

Cade feels the softness of Morgan's lips as they graze his face, aware, also of the barely perceptible touch of her body as she leans against him to accept *bisou bisou*.   There is a feeling of guilt at the enjoyment of his lips on her and the fleeting press of her body against his-he is stealing pleasure in the guise of an innocent greeting. In the instant in time that it takes his lips to graze across her soft, warm skin, ritual has become personal, and Jon Cade feels a charge of desire that is new and disturbing at the same time.

Cade's chest muscles are tense and tingling from Morgan's touch, and he quickly turns his attention to Carson. "Carson! You made it! How nice to see you." He grasps Carson's outstretched hand; the ceremonial ritual makes him feel manly.

"Glad to be here Jon-good to see you."

Still smiling, Cade asks, "What have you two been up to? Behaving yourselves I hope."

Morgan laughs. "I like your friend. He's good in the kitchen. No food or supplies? Have you been shopping?"

"Oh, Leda and Martin seemed intent on going to market. Made me feel a third wheel so I went to the museum. They should be along shortly."

Third wheel?   Carson thinks he will
have to take more seriously what Morgan
has told him.

Carson and Morgan are sitting across
from each other, drinking the last of
the Perrier from their wine glasses. The
remains of a Parisian feast–plates of
various sizes, wine glasses, water, and
smaller ones for the calvados, butter and
sauce dishes, used napkins, salt and pepper mills, and candles–clutter the table
between them. Cade and Martin have gone
down into the courtyard to smoke, leaving Carson and Morgan to help Leda with
the clean up.

For the dinner festivities, Morgan has
exchanged her jeans and sweater for a
sleeveless black dress with a generous
décolleté. There is a gold and silver
Breitling on her left wrist: a simple
silver chain encircles the other. Around

her neck, on a matching chain, hang two thin circles-one gold, the other silver. The ring finger of her right hand is adorned with a gold band with diamonds set in an inlay of silver.

Morgan leans forward, pouring the remaining Perrier in his glass, and the deep plunge of her neckline gives him a view of the smooth skin between the swell of her breasts, and he is aware of a warm dusty rose like scent that is wafting from that very delectable place. He would like very much to kiss her there…like very much to feel his lips on her skin.

She sees Carson looking at her. Smiling, she returns the favor. She likes his eyes. They communicate openness, depth, and some secrecy too. She remembers them squeezed close in the doorway; it was not planned, but it was not an accident.

"Quite a meal."

"It was a feast."

"Really fun, Carson. But, I want to know what you're thinking."

"I was thinking of the dinner conversation.

"I really like Cade and Leda. I'm not sure about Martin. But, for sure, they're in a muddle."

"Jon and Leda definitely not in sync."

"Yes. And, I believe you are right; Martin's attention is very flattering to Leda."

"Indeed. Their entire conversation wasn't say what you mean, mean what you say. I wish Cade was more tuned in to what's going on."

"It's sad."

"They may be shocked at what happens."

"I don't think whatever is going on is happening because they're married."

"I agree. But, marriage…ah…intensifies the brew."

Leda yells from the kitchen, "Hey you guys! Stop whatever you are doing and finish clearing the table."

They both laugh. Getting up, Carson removes some plates from the table. Morgan does the same, grabbing some glasses.

Carson reaches the doorway first and waits. Morgan squeezes in next to him. Careful not to drop the plates balanced between them, they lean toward each other. She feels his wine laden breath on her. *I want to get drunk on that.* Morgan feels Carson's lips against hers, warm and deliciously rough, sending warm waves throughout her body. It is over too soon.

They gaze into each other's eyes, leaning as close as possible.

"What are you doing out there? Must I do everything?"

In the kitchen Leda starts bossing them, and they obey her commands like two guilty children. The cleaning comes to a halt with the return of Jon and Martin. The two men seem to be friends now-buddies rather than adversaries vying for Leda's attention. Carson allows that perhaps sharing a smoke will do that.

"Carson! I'm going to walk Martin back to his hotel. Get your coat, and I'll do the same for you." Carson can tell Cade is tipsy, and that it has amped up his bonhomie. "The girls can finish up here."

"I want to do that too. Leda. Let's walk the guys home."

Leda turns from the sink, a look of displeasure, perhaps, Morgan thinks, trying to also convey long suffering, etched on her lovely face. "No. No, I want to get this done." Then, looking at Cade, "Besides I want to get to bed. Try to be quiet when you get back."

Morgan darts into the bedroom she is using, returning just as quickly slipping into a faded Levi jacket. Carson grabs his jacket from the sofa, and, after giving Leda hugs and kisses, they crowd through the door and clamber down the stairs to the courtyard.

It has finally rained; the cobblestones glisten with wetness from the brief downpour. The mugginess is gone, and the night air is fresh and clean. To Carson everything feels brand-new. Outside on the street it is quiet until they arrive at the intersection of the Boulevards

Saint Germain and *Raspail* where crowds of people are on the move. The bar at the intersection is overflowing. It becomes quiet again as the four head in the direction of the *Madison.* Martin pulls Morgan ahead of Jon and Carson, showing off his expertise as a banker by providing her with a lecture on the inner workings of ATMs.

Turning to Carson, Cade sighs. "I feel sour."

Carson thinks of sour grapes. "Like a bad taste in your mouth?"

"More like my whole body. It's like something is on the way to spoiling."

"Does this involve Leda?"

Cade nods. "I was looking forward to this trip. You know spending time with Leda-museums, eating at good restaurants, taking the train from here to there. It hasn't happened. She hardly seemed to notice me tonight…." His voice trails off, leaving a sad silence between them.

"We were getting to know Morgan, and when we found out she was going to be in France when we were, Leda suggested we invite her to stay at the apartment we rented in Paris. I guess I was a bit jealous…I wanted Leda to myself. I told Leda I wanted to think about it, but she went ahead and invited Morgan anyway. I'm not really sure how it happened, maybe I was mad, and maybe I thought that if she can do it, I could, too. I don't know. Anyway, when you e-mailed me about getting your license, and your celebration trip to France, I invited you.

"Just after we took off from SEATAC, she told me she had invited Martin. It's been very weird between us ever since. That's why you are staying in a hotel. Originally the guest room was yours…until Morgan entered the mix. Martin is at the *Madison* because, as he made clear, I always stay in the Madison when in Paris."

"What's going on, Jon?"

"Well, Leda hasn't said so in so many words, but I think she's angry because she thinks I'm trying to get you and Morgan together."

Creepy. Morgan and I are two pawns in a marital fuck-up. What a way to meet. Carson thinks there may be another explanation for Martin's presence in Paris.

"How does Martin fit into all this?"

"I'm not really sure. I guess he's an old friend of ours."

Carson realizes they have reached the outskirts of the Paris nightlife around *Saint Germain des Prés*; they are engulfed in a mélange of Parisian revelers. As they cross *rue des Saints Pères*, they rejoin Morgan and Martin. Just before, Carson puts his arm on Cade's, slowing him down.

"Pay attention, Jon."

"Martin wants to stop at *Aux Deux Magots* for a calvados." Morgan's statement seems a warning aimed at Carson.

Cade likes the idea. "Yes. Perfect."

Carson follows Morgan's prompt. "Listen. Why don't you have your *digestif*? I've had too much to drink. Besides, I need to be in my bed."

"Yeah. You two guys enjoy your calvados. I'll walk Carson to his hotel." Both men look stunned.

Martin tries to be clever. "What! Have we missed something? Do you need a chaperone?"

Morgan laughs. "I'll call if I do."

Cade is more serious. "But, Morgan, how will you get back to the apartment? Should I come and get you, or meet you someplace?"

"That's sweet, Jon. Go ahead and have your drink with Martin, then get him to his hotel. I'll see you back at the apartment." She is already heading toward *Saint Michel*; Carson follows after her. On the other side of the street, they slow, turning back; Morgan waves. The two men dutifully wave, and then slowly turn into the crowd milling around *Deux Magots*.

Morgan slips her arm through his.

Walking arm in arm as a couple fits the feeling of familiarity she feels toward Carson. *I can let my hair down with him and be myself, worry less about being judged*. Actually, she has felt this way ever since they met.

"Let's walk to *Place Maubert*."

"Fine." He likes the feel of Morgan's breast against his arm. "I think we need to share a bit of our backgrounds with each other."

"You do? A bit of background info, huh."

"Yeah. A hundred words. You go first."

"I was born in Santa Fe-no brothers or sisters. My mother died when I was eighteen. When I finished junior high school, my father sent me to school in Europe… Switzerland-he was Swiss. Before I went to the Sorbonne, I was an undergraduate at Mills College in Oakland. You know… California. I returned to the States to Johns Hopkins for my M.D.

"My dad died about ten years ago. He was hiking in the Sierras, near Tuolumne Meadows. He was never found."

Carson nods, shaking his head, saying nothing. Then, "How do you come to terms with that…how do you get closure?"

"You don't. He's in a small crawl space in my mind. I just don't go there."

Carson nods again, this time in silence.

"You?" she asks.

"Sacramento. My parents were originally from Virginia–Arlington. They split up for a while and my father moved to Sacramento. I was born after my mother rejoined him. I have two brothers, one younger and one older.

"My parents are still living; they moved to Cardiff-by-the-Sea. As my brothers and I got older, we drifted away. I just stopped coming home as much, sleeping over at my older brother's place, and then my own apartment. Then I was on my own. I don't think my dad noticed. After my injury, he concentrated on my younger brother."

Morgan tightens her grip on him. Then: "What about your mom?"

"I should see her more often."

They reach *Boulevard Saint Michel,* and cross in a crowd. On the other side they cross *rue de la Harpe*, sifting through the stream of people who have just crossed from the *Cluny* side of *Saint Michel*.

Slipping his arm around Morgan's waist, he guides her to the margin of the crowd, a quiet space near the buildings. Anticipating his intentions Morgan lets herself be guided into his arms, then his embrace.

Morgan feels Carson's lips against hers, sending warm waves throughout her body.

They gaze into each other's eyes.

"Again."

He kisses her again.

Morgan pulls Carson against her, arms wrapping around him. The warmth of his chest against her ignites a fiery passion. She feels his hand on the small of her back, pressing her closer.

Carson disengages himself, again seeking her eyes. Her eyes gaze into his, but her attention seems lazy. A faint smile fades and returns when her lips part and then come back together. The dusty rose scent is between them.

The crowd suddenly swirls around them, jostling them, making them laugh as they untangle from each other, and head toward *Place Maubert*. Maubert is busy, but they find a table at the brassiere in front of the small park that is the apex of the confluence of streets coming together at *Place Maubert* and order Perriers.

Morgan sighs. "I'm buzzed."

"Me, too. It's not totally the wine."

"Yes. Same for me."

Running her hand through her hair, she sighs again.

Carson holds out his hand, and she takes it. "Eros carouses Paris tonight."

To Morgan, Carson's eyes seem very clear, but there is weariness there, too. Perhaps it is his profession. Perhaps it is an awareness of the absurdness that lurks so near most of the time. Whatever it is, she thinks it makes him attractive to women, because they can see the weariness and feel his sense of the absurd, and then they see him turn his total attention to them; he can suspend his weariness of the world and pay attention to them.

It has happened to her. His gaze seems a mix of interest and curiosity, so intense that she feels it engulf her, drawing her into his influence. Involuntarily she leans toward him.

"You make me feel good."

"I'm glad. I really feel good, too. You know we started as pawns in the marital discord between Jon and Leda Cade. However, left to our own devices something pretty wonderful is happening."

Carson watches Morgan run her hand through her hair. Pensively she takes a sip of her Perrier. "Will Eros be having coffee at some café tomorrow morning?"

"He'll be sleeping in…but we should."

"Ah. Yes, the morning after. Where?"

"Do you have a suggestion?"

"Yes. Let's meet in the Luxembourg Gardens. We can have a coffee and then walk…or sit in the sun…or both."

"Great. There's a café near the Senate. *Rendezvous* there at ten…Ok?"

"Yes."   She sees Carson frown. "What?"

"We should exchange phone numbers."

"Good idea."   Then it's her turn to frown. "I didn't bring my mobile."

"Not a problem." Carson pulls a matchbox and a pen from his backpack, and, after dumping out the matches, writes his number in the empty box and slips it back in its cover. "Here. At least you have mine."

Morgan takes the matchbox, glancing at it quickly before slipping it in a pocket of her jacket. In various shades of blue and gray stylized smoke waifs from a pipe with the words *Tabac pour pipe* under it. *Melange Aromatique* runs down the left edge with *Allumettes* printed in small letters at the bottom.

"Nice. When I see, Ari and Blanca I'll use one of their phones to call you."

"Call anytime."

There is a pause in their conversation, and the space between them is filled with the late night sounds of *Place Maubert*. Carson realizes that their arrangement for morning coffee has changed the nature of their new and brief encounter; it has extended it, giving it a future. It has also altered the direction of their evening.

Morgan crosses her legs, brushing against his; there is brief, lingering contact before they both shift away.

She breaks the silence. "I take it you can find your way back to your hotel from here."

"That I can." Carson puts a Euro in the empty ashtray. "Walk me across the street."

They stop at the entrance to *rue Maître Albert*. "You remind me of one of Modigliani's women."

Morgan's face becomes warm as a current of excitement flows through her. "That's nice. Which one?"

"Oh, Jeanne Hubuterne," he lies.

She thinks she knows the one he is talking about. She doesn't think it looks like her, but his thinking she does is romantic. Passion stirs in her.

"Jean Hubuterne dressed."

"Yes."

A buzz vibrates gently throughout Morgan's body. She lets her head drop back, gazes at the sky, and then back to Carson.

"Modigliani painted nudes, too."

Carson's words, meant to be complimentary and uttered without reflection have changed the mood between them, and Morgan has responded in kind. He feels, more than knowing, a shift has taken place between them; desire has become a possibility. *Eros is still carousing.*

"Uh. That's true. Morgan. Come back to my hotel with me. I want you to."

Morgan's response is to take Carson's arm and push him down *rue Maître Albert*. It is quiet on the narrow street; the lobby of the *Notre Dame* is empty and there are only two or three patrons in the small bar on the right halfway down the street. They turn into *Place Montebello*, basking in the glow of *Notre Dame*, where the restaurants are still busy, and head to *Degrés de Notre Dame*. They avoid the small restaurant, there are still some patrons finishing up their dinners, and enter the small hallway and stairs to the hotel. Morgan waits while Carson goes into the restaurant for the key.

Inside the small, plain but comfortable room, Morgan throws her jacket over a chair and kicks off her shoes before coming to Carson.

He leans close and kisses her as he reaches around her, pulling the zipper of her black dress down-slowly, very slowly, his fingers dragging across her back, so smooth and warm. Then he pulls the straps away from her shoulders until it slips down her body to the floor-after Morgan wiggles it past her hips. Then his arms are around her again to unhook the lacy black bra. She laughs-"In the front."

Next the miniscule black lacy briefs are slipped past her hips and down her legs to be sent flying by a flick of her foot.

In the cool silence of the room she removes Carson's clothes. The white shirt comes off, then the jeans. She stops pulling on his gray and white pin-stripped shorts long enough to put her hand on him, urging along his growing excitement.

Carson runs his fingers through her hair, over the tiny scars while Morgan draws her fingers over him.

"Oh! That feels so good."

"Keep you hand there."

Morgan falls on the bed, holding out her arms to him. The sheets feel cool on her backside, and she wriggles on them to intensify the feeling. Coming to her, he kneels between her legs, leaning forward and kissing her, moving his hand between her legs until his fingers brush soft curls–lazily coiled. Then there is a pause as he leans back. The anticipation is so overwhelming that Morgan can only gasp. She feels his hand between her legs and opens, moving her hips. *Hurry. Now. Now!* She feels his body on her, their eyes meet–she can feel him in her.

"Ah!"

He sighs, "Morgan."

She gasps. "Oh! That's good. Soooo good."

Now, physically, Morgan feels her moorings slipping, and then the delicious anticipation of losing track of time and place, the blurring of all except the desire to continue.

He feels the pressure of Morgan's legs against him, wrapped around him. Morgan's eyes are closed; there is a faint blush on her cheeks. A frown crosses her face, only to disappear back into smoothness. Her eyelids flutter and he sees brown with flashes of green. Then her eyes open, and she stares at him, looking surprised, before smiling.

"Don't stop."

He feels himself approaching the point where control and volition cease to have meaning. He feels near a point where he will no longer be separate from Morgan. He is aware of an increasing tension that desires to both continue indefinitely and to let go.

"Carson!"

He tries to hold back, to anchor himself, to stop time, but in the grip of her passion, he is carried ahead.

"We made lovely romance. This evening will always be part of me…."

She has left the bed, and, facing away from him, is dressing. "Yes. It was so nice…so special. Do it again?"

"Yes-a beginning without end. You don't have to leave."

She doesn't answer. Carson had been very attentive almost to the point of hesitancy. But the result had been delicious. Twice. Her entire body is still vibrating with the memory of their lovemaking. Yet, there is the hint of shyness. *Post-coital regret*? She thinks not. Proof? Truth? If they will still love each other in the morning she wants to find out in the brightness of Luxemburg Gardens.

The black dress drops over her and into place. Still in bare feet, she goes into the bathroom, closing the door.

Carson's thoughts flit back and forth from their love making to the quiet darkness of the hotel room. His hands still have the memory of her body. He remembers her legs wrapped around him, hands on him. Each time, as she announced her orgasm, grabbing for a pillow to muffle her cries. He will never forget, never forget this night. He will never forget Morgan. It seems that gravity rules their brand new relationship; there is no need to tinker. Perhaps tomorrow there will be talk.

He hears the toilet. She comes over and sits on the edge of the bed. "Yes I do. Bourgeois respectability. We've created enough mischief. And, I don't want Jon and Leda to freak out and do something stupid."

She leans down, pursing her lips. He gives her a kiss, a quick one because she pulls away quickly.

"Coffee in Luxembourg tomorrow?"

"Yes. That's our plan."

Stopping at the door, she slips into her shoes and pulls on her jacket. Then she is gone.

Chapter Two

Reunion

He remembers. He remembers her smile. He
remembers her smooth bronzed skin, and
dark brown eyes flecked with green. He
remembers the taste, scent, and feel of
her.

He had arrived at the small café in the
Jardin du Luxembourg a few minutes before
the agreed upon time settling at a table,
the dappled morning light creating a pattern of sun and shade on its bright green
top, with a view of the senate straight
ahead, and Marie de Medici's reflection
pool on the right. The gravel paths were
filling with strollers, and through the
trees, he could see Parisians positioning
themselves around the lake in anticipation of a bright and sunny day.

Forty minutes later Morgan entered through the gate on rue de *Medicis* (he had used the one off *Place de Rostand*) the essence of Parisian chic in blue straight legged tight jeans, a black scoop-necked t-shirt under a skinny belted leather jacket-sleeves pushed up-a leather purse matching the belt and black Puma flats and giving him a wave as she climbed the steps near the reflection pool before reaching the table where she leaned close to give him a kiss on the lips then pulled her waiting chair close to him before sitting.

For a while they seemed content to sit close, sip their *au laits* from large ceramic cups and munch on fresh croissants. Morgan finally broke the not unpleasant silence.

"Montebello was still busy when I left and decided to walk back, but I saw a taxi and changed my mind. A couple of tiny lights had been left on, but it was mainly dark, dark and quiet. Leda and Jon were in their own rooms, doors closed. I tiptoed into the study quietly closing the door. It was quiet the rest of the night, except for a couple of times when Jon staggered down the hall to the bathroom to puke.

"When I got up, Jon was still *hors de combat,* but Leda was up and came into my room to watch me pack. I think she had figured things out, but didn't say anything. When I told her I was meeting you for breakfast, she gave me that long suffering look of hers, and said, Well, be sure you don't miss your train."

Carson remembers piggybacking on her story. "You know, if I could do it over, I'd do the same thing."

"I would too. And, if you hadn't asked, I would have followed you to your room."

"I don't want this to be a one of a kind happening."

"Well, in its own way it is, but I want it to evolve and continue."

Morgan had stopped with a shake of her head, "And…I just don't know what that means. For now, anyway." And that became the state of their affair after the first night.

Feeling the press of time, they wandered around the lake, people watching, and then down *Saint Michel* to *San Germain* where they decided that Morgan would return to the Cade's place alone, and Carson would show up after she was on the way to Geneva. As they parted Morgan pulled the matchbox from her purse promising to call as soon as she was in Geneva. Morgan had not called. He had asked Cade for her phone number. Of course, it was the one for her mobile: *Leave a message. I will return your call.*

After passing his licensing exam, he moved out of his apartment near the UCLA campus, selling all his furniture, and books. The invitation from Jon Cade re-fined his plans. For the two weeks before leaving for France, he stayed with some friends on Martel near the Melrose, prac-ticing for café culture in Paris by hang-ing out at Café Luna. After leaving Los Angeles, he crashed at a friend's place in Berkeley before leaving for Paris, so that returning there from his trip felt like coming home.

Back in Berkeley he called Bernie Lane (There was no listing for Blanca Lane in the phone book.) who did not return his calls, forcing him to become philosophical. Two possibilities. The first, and most complex, is that she has not been able to wrap her mind around them as a twosome in terms of her life. More simply put, she can't fit him into her life. The second hunch is that when she talked to her women friends–Ari and Blanca–they either talked her out of continuing, or convinced her to slow down.

It's the details that keeping him busy, make him feel off-kilter. Still…things are falling into place. His Chevy Astro, bought used two weeks ago after his return from France, is parked nearby in the lot under the BART station. In his backpack are the keys to his new digs–a studio on the property of a large Claremont Avenue house.

He stirs his lukewarm cappuccino—lukewarm because he forgot, again, to ask for it to be hot—and watches the crowd on College Avenue from his table in front of Peaberry's. Soon after his arrival in the Bay Area, Carson made a few phone calls, and was surprised to quickly have three patients scheduled to start psychotherapy.

Enter Gloria Belknap. Gloria has a doctorate, a Psy.D., from one of the numerous private schools in the area and an M.S., in Marriage and Family Therapy.

She has not left him alone since he agreed, too quickly, to meet her at Peaberry's and take a look at her office. *I have made a mistake.* His hurry to secure an office, prompted by the three quick referrals, short-circuited his judgment leading to what quickly became an untenable situation with Gloria. Phone calls and e-mails each with endless questions and never-ending suppositions lacking the concreteness of reality landed in his in-box and lurked in his voice mail.

She has put him on the defensive, and
he feels he is always trying to explain
himself. What is most disturbing is her
vacillation between being suspicious and
questioning and being very friendly and
helpful…sometimes even flirty.

His iPhone rings. It's Gloria Belknap.

"Hey, Gloria."

"Hi. Where are you?"

"In front of Peaberry's."

"Oh good I've just parked…be right
there."

At their first meeting, Carson was surprised by how much space she commanded-
physically and interpersonally. She is a
big woman with a pretty face framed by
short blond hair flipping up at the ends.
Her uniform, always in subtle, complemen-
tary colors, is a voluminous skirt, silk
shirt with a collar with long pointed ends
under a long vest and a large purse hanging over her shoulder. She has a diamond
in each ear, and always has her fingers
and arms adorned with multiple rings and
bracelets. She flows rather than moves,

accompanied by tinkling sounds. Tinkling sounds, which he hears now.

"Oh, hi, Carson." Moving the chair, she sits beside him. Close.

"Hey, Gloria."

"Get me a mocha, would you?"

Dutifully Carson starts to head inside.

"To go…and whipped cream. And, get a paper cup for your cap."

Back at the table a sweet scent hovers between them.

"Did you leave any broken hearts in L.A?"

"A few Baristas at Starbucks."

"Carson! Were you hitting on the young girls?"

"I was just joking, Gloria."

"Oh." Gloria takes a sip of the mocha, and then fits the lid over the paper cup. "Have you heard of BAKS?"

"Backs?"

"Bay Area Kohut Society. A half dozen old-time Berkeley shrinks have been meeting for years. Now they've decided to make themselves lifetime members and accept applications for membership. They'll accept a few as charter members, before opening to general members. I want to be a charter member…very prestigious."

Boring. "I take it they practice self psychology."

"Psychoanalytic for sure, but I think several of them knew Kohut."

Carson nods that he is listening, and takes a sip of his lukewarm cappuccino.

"Say. Would you write me a letter of recommendation? I could use some recommendations."

"Gloria. I just met you."

"I certainly have the qualifications. I have a doctorate in psychology, I'm an MFT, and a part-time faculty member at Cal State."

"I don't have any problem with your qualifications. It's just that I haven't known you long enough, to, ah, to make a statement about you professionally."

Gloria frowns at him, her clear blue eyes staring. She says nothing. Then retrieving her purse from under her chair, says, "Come on. I'll show you my office."

Gloria's office is spacious and comfortable. They agree on a rental fee, and the hours he will use her office. On the way over she had asked for a copy of his license, and he asked her what license she used. Her answer was brusque. "My MFT license." Clearly she did not like his question. It is easy to rub her the wrong way.

"OK. I'll get you some keys, and a copy of the agreement. I'll give you a ring when they're ready, and we can finish things up.

"By the way, will you be in the office tomorrow evening?"

"I have a seven and an eight."

"Could I use your nine o'clock slot?"

"If it's one time only, I don't see why not."

"Good." Smiling, she leans back in her leather chair, the only one in the office-when he first saw it, he decided not to use it; what was good enough for his patients would be good enough for him.

"What about Paris? Any conquests?"

"I did meet a woman."

"Was she French?"

"American. I met her at a dinner party with some other Americans. We, I think, hit it off-we both seemed comfortable with each other, and the time flew by."

"What happened?"

Carson shrugs and pulls on his ear. *No details.* "Well, we had a great dinner, and walked around Paris until late. It was very nice. We decided to have breakfast in the morning, and we said goodbye before she left for Geneva that afternoon. I gave her my mobile number. We would talk. But…she didn't call."

"She hasn't called?"

"No."

"Did she give you her number?"

"She didn't bring her mobile. She said she would use one of her friend's phones to call."

Losing interest, Gloria looks at her watch. "Got to get going. Walk me to my car."

Leaving her office, they hurry across Shafter and into the BART parking lot. Carson realizes that the most disturbing thing about Gloria is the unpredictability of her moods.

"I hope they keep a level playing field for acceptance into BAKS."

"I would expect them to."

Gloria shows him a smirk to let him know how silly he is. Then, "Well, they've already taken in some young doctor who has just landed here from Seattle."

Holy Shit! "She's moved here from Seattle?"

"Yes. She's living at Point Reyes Station until her house off Tunnel is ready. When she's here, she stays with two young women at their place in the Rockridge." At the mention of the two women, Gloria raises her eyebrows, sending a You know what I mean message. "They've been seen shopping together at Whole Foods."

"Where is her practice?"

"She's looking for a building to buy. Until that happens she is using Bernard Lane's office, over in North Berkeley on The Alameda. Bernie is one of the founders of BAKS."

"You are a font of knowledge."

Gloria laughs, high pitched and brittle. "Yes. Knowledge is power."

"You must be well connected."

Again, the raised eyebrows: "You better believe it."

"This new doctor. Have you gleaned a name for her?"

"She's a foreigner. It's Alar. You're asking a lot of questions."

"Just getting to know you." Carson is quite sure Gloria, being a human GPS device, has located Morgan in the East Bay. He tries to conceal his jubilation and be protective at the same time. "I don't think this new person will be a problem for you."

"Oh no…not at all. I always get what I want. I just want them to play fair."

"Yes. It makes sense."

Taking her keys out of her purse, she proffers her cheek, and he pecks at it. "Well, see you tomorrow."

"Tomorrow?"

"Remember. I'm using your nine o'clock slot. Be out on time!"

Carson squeezes his Astro into a space between a Lexus SUV and a Toyota Prius. Shutting off the engine he relaxes as the sun, newly emergent after burning off the gray morning cloud layer, fills the cab with its warmth. The nose of the cab is facing across Ashby at the Chevron Station that dominates one of the busy corners of the Telegraph, Ashby intersection. In his rear view mirror he can see his destination, Whole Foods.

Gloria's information about Morgan had thrown him into a surreal landscape. He had immediately began to search, finding there was no Morgan Alar in Point Reyes Station-so much for Gloria's far flung information web. He could not find her with his White Pages app, and she was not in the Alameda County Medical Association Directory. Of course, without a last name for Ari, he could not find her. He had left another message for Bernie Lane, but he had not replied. Then he slowed down, beginning to feel like a stalker. He had decided to make a few expeditions to Whole Foods, and, that failing, he would call Bernie Lane again.

The cab of the Astro is heating up, and Carson doesn't like ruminating over past events. He has a short list; he'll do a quick shopping and then check out Ikea. Leaving the windows open, he heads to the store. Near the entrance there is an area of tables, some filled with individuals eating something bought from the store. Closer to the door, there are some displays of fruit, vegetables, and flowers. The shopping carts are in two rows to the left of the sliding glass doors.

His mobile rings. It's Gloria. "Hey, Gloria."

"Where are you?"

"Whole Foods."

"It should be easy for you to meet me at Peaberry's in an hour-I have a two-hour break. We can have coffee, and I can give you the keys to the office and go over some details with you. OK?"

Carson needs the keys to the office. "OK. Peaberry's in an hour."

"Oh Carson? You still there?"

"Yes."

"Let's do dinner Friday. I have a gift certificate for Café Rouge. Everything will be paid for." His ear fills with her laughter.

"Let's talk about it at Peaberry's."

"What's wrong with now?"

"Give me some space, Gloria."

There is a silence between them. Then: "OK. Bye." She is gone.

Slipping his phone in a front pocket of his Levis, Carson goes to the queue and pulls out a green shopping cart. *What am I going to do about Gloria?*

Once inside Whole Foods, Carson finds himself part of a beehive of activity-food in Berkeley is very important and shopping a serious endeavor. For an instant he is like a deer caught in the headlights, and then, for self-defense if nothing else, he merges into the flow of urban food gathering. Whole Foods, as opposed to Safeway or Berkeley Bowl, stocks Black Current oil–he will be able to replenish his supply–and makes his first stop the vitamin section. He is not sure where to search, ending up in the middle aisle, near the men's section, and the women's section. His eyes rove up and down the shelves; he thinks that instead of here, the Black Current might be in a section for skin. He sees two women discussing a container of something in front of the women's section. Both are a bit younger than he, one with short blond hair the other, light brown. They are a study in contrasts, defying an easy description of their connection.

The woman with the light brown hair, falling plainly to her shoulders, seems tired or subdued for some reason. She is

not wearing any make-up, which accentu-
ates her clear, brown eyes. The simplicity
continues with a black sleeveless dress
with a V-neck, its hem falling below her
knees. Her only jewelry is a necklace,
a dark pewter chain joined to the narrow
ends of a gold ellipse. A plain white
sweater is bunched under the strap of a
large black purse.

The blond, her sunglasses pushed up on
the top of her head, is wearing a denim
mini skirt and a light blue T-shirt with
the image of a Greek flag on the front.
Underneath, in mock Greek letters is *I
Found Love in Greece*. Silver bracelets
rub against each other on each of her
slim wrists. Her backpack is in their
cart.

He is close enough to hear what they
are saying. The blond, holding the bottle, replaces it while saying, "Well.
Let's ask Morgan. She's the doctor."
Like a light breeze a whisper of craziness briefly envelops him, propel-
ling him to take a path that makes no

sense.   Rotating his cart a hundred and eighty degrees, he heads toward the dairy section, turning right in front of it. Slowly he wheels past each aisle, searching the shoppers in each–a man pushing an empty cart, staring.   Looking for… what?   He reaches the last aisle before the wine and cheese section, intent on his mission.   And there, alone at the end of the aisle, in front of the olive oil section is…Morgan.   Wearing tight blue jeans and a white hooded, short-waisted sweatshirt over a black T-shirt hanging below the hoodie, she has pushed the end of her cart against the shelves, and, leaning over the end of her basket, is staring at the numerous bottles of olive oil.   She has put her leather purse in the cart, its color matching her black European style shoes.

Since their night and day in Paris, Carson has imagined countless reunions including the lobby of the Berkeley Repertory Theater or Davies Hall, leaving the Pacific Film Archive Theater after a late evening film, or on the Bear Valley Trail at Point Reyes. Or, an East Bay trail, the Sea View for example. And, more in keeping with an It's over, theme, discovering her with her new boyfriend at an upscale Berkeley restaurant, or one of the French bistros in the City-Café Claude, for example. Each imaginary situation contains enough pizzazz to create an emotionally laden conversation leading to their reunion. He never imagined the olive oil section of a grocery store, and now, even with his Modigliani woman the length of a grocery store aisle from him his response is subdued. In fact, he cannot muster the fantasies of his ideal woman whose likeness, thanks to Modigliani, rests in a compartment of his backpack. Instead she is, turning toward him, the woman he met and fell in love with in Paris-in sum, the real Morgan.

Morgan is looking for a bargain: a gallon of tasty oil that doesn't cost an arm and a leg. She is wondering if

the Whole Foods label meets the criteria
when a hint of motion on the periphery
of her vision draws her attention down
the aisle. *Oh my God! Am I saved…or ruined*? A smiling Carson Arrowsmith, in a
black T-shirt and jeans, is approaching
her, his gray and red cross trainers
squeaking plaintively on the highly polished linoleum floor. To her surprise he
seems thinner than at their Paris meeting; his hair also seems shorter, more
spiked. And, most interesting, his face
lacks the ravages of sun damage that
she remembers from their first meeting.
Where was my head…?

She lets out a shout. "Carson! I can't
believe…."

"Morgan…." He takes hold of her outstretched hands, letting himself fall
momentarily into the depths of her dark
greenish brown eyes. There, instead of
her secrets, he finds a reflection of his
own nascent desire.

His hands are warm, and smooth, and she
feels giddy in their grasp. The feeling

is the same as in Paris—a willingness to be moved by him.

Still holding her hands, Carson kisses her lightly on both cheeks. Her skin is soft, warm, and each kiss seems to release the smell of dusty roses and summer heat. Carson feels Morgan's pursed lips brush lightly against him as they complete the ritual of *bisou bisou*. The ritual of salutation gives them time to take a deep breath and gather their wits—then they are in each other's arms. While not as fierce as Paris when they, with a mixture of reluctance and passion, parted, the time between this embrace and that one is erased. Carson anticipates the feel of Morgan's lips against his, but she pulls away disengaging her self. "Ari, Blanca. This is Carson."

Morgan's two friends have found them. The woman with the light brown hair, falling plainly to her shoulders is the first to speak: "Ah, the conquest."

The blond offers him her hand. "I'm Ari."

"Pleased to meet you Ari." He nods to Blanca who studies him, and then smiling, says. "Well, well, it seems all roads lead to Whole Foods."

"How about having coffee…perhaps dinner?"

Ari smiles. "Are you inviting us to dinner?"

"I am. Why not? But, Morgan, coffee when shopping is finished?"

Now, it's Blanca's turn, and she seems pleased to say, "I don't think so. We're shopping for the weekend at Stinson."

Morgan intervenes. "Blanca is right. We leave for Stinson after we finish here. I won't be back until Monday morning."

Morgan and Carson stare at each other, then Morgan continues. "But listen. Blanca and Ari: You finish up here while Carson and I have coffee. We'll go to Roma, and you can pick me up there."

Blanca and Ari stare at Morgan. Ari smiles and nods. Blanca grabs Morgan's cart and retreats down the aisle. Ari follows, and Carson and Morgan are alone.

Morgan grabs Carson's arm. "Let's go."

The afternoon sun still warms the small, paved terrace that is the entrance to Roma, and Morgan settles in at a table with her back to Ashby, waiting for Carson to bring their coffees. There is a low cement wall with a wooden bench attached to it that separates the street from the coffee house. The top of the wall is a planter, filled with neatly trimmed Salvia. Patrons choosing not to sit on the wooden benches can take their drinks while sitting in black metal chairs that match the round tables scattered about the terrace.

From her purse, next to her on the wooden bench, Morgan removes a small compact and a lipstick, and, using the compact's mirror, applies some color to her lips. Still using the mirror she runs her fingers through her dark hair, producing flashes of red; her fingers leave a trail of spikes, some remaining, some collapsing back into the rest of the tousled hair. She has often wondered that if there was a reunion would the magic of their first meeting repeat itself. She knows it has. In an instant Carson has landed…smack in her current life-well planned, well ordered, well practiced-without any hint of its affect…on her…on her life.

Waiting in line, Carson watches Morgan, mirror in hand, do some fixing up.   In less time than between when he saw her bending over her cart in front of the olive oil and kissing her, they are again drawn to each other with a trip wire of passion hovering about them. Carson places one *café au lait*-in a slender glass with a curved glass handle-in front of Morgan, then sitting across from her, puts his in front of him.

Morgan pats the bench next to her, and, coffee in hand, he moves next to her.

Carson nods and smiles.   "I cannot believe this. I mean this is so great-finding you again. I had not given up…but the odds seemed so great…until I saw you at Whole Foods it seemed such a long time since we said goodbye at the train station."

"When I saw you, I thought I was going fly apart at the seams with happiness. As soon as we parted, I missed you. I felt regretful. Strangely, I believe I experienced our parting as a loss. I think I have been grieving." She frowns.

"You could have called."

"Carson, that's just it; I couldn't."

"Couldn't…?"

"I lost the matchbox…."

"Morgan…."

"Honest to God. I did! Hear me out."

Carson takes a sip of his *au lait*, and nods.

"That night, when I got back to Jon and Leda's, I put the matchbox on the table next to my bed. In the morning I debated whether to put it in my purse or my cosmetics bag. I finally decided to put it in my cosmetics bag in my carryon.

And there it stayed when I left Paris, and it was there when I got to Geneva. Every time I used my cosmetic bag I saw it.   Then, the morning after we arrived in Athens, it was gone.   I looked everywhere-even had Ari and Blanca take a look.   Gone."

"And, I'm supposed to believe this?"

"Carson!   You have to!   Just before we said goodbye, and you told me you'd be waiting for me wherever you took your coffee, I told myself: I'll call him from Athens…he should be in Nice…just like we planned. I should have called as soon as I met Ari and Blanca in Geneva."

Rummaging in his backpack, Carson pulls a matchbook from it. Plain white, it boasts a red bull's eye with Best Yet floating in the center of it. After more rummaging Carson comes up with a pen, and writes on the inside of the matchbook.

He hands it to her. She opens it. On the inside Carson has written in his careful script: Call me. Anytime. Beneath his neat signature is his mobile number. Morgan stuffs it in her jeans pocket.

"Does this mean you believe me?"

"Yes."

Morgan laughs. Then. "Can we go inside? I'm a bit chilly."

Taking their drinks, they go inside, finding two wooden stools at the small marble bar next to the cash register and espresso machine and its paraphernalia. The bar curves around toward a pay phone, an emergency exit, and the entrance to the restroom. Typically Berkeley, there are posters advertising a range of activities from small theater groups, alternative health activities, and musical events on the wall, and postcard sized advertisements on the counter underneath them. Next to the phone there is a metal shelf with more cards. Carson also notes that the *wifi* is free.

Morgan observes that, except for a light splash of red blush on each cheek, his complexion is smooth and clear. Morgan decides that Carson's eyes are hazel

in color. She recalls that hazel eyes
are due to a combination of a Rayleigh
scattering–named after a Lord Rayleigh
and having to do with the scattering of
light particles–and a moderate amount
of melanin in the iris's anterior bor-
der layer. They are very pretty and appear to change color from time to time.
Light brown to green and sometimes even
gray.   Carson is wearing his watch–G-
SHOCK–in red on the silver rim–on his
left wrist, and she can see the seconds
languidly, as if they are liquid, count-
ing toward the next minute. She assumes
he is right handed. She is struck that
it seems but a few days ago that they
met for the first time. She thinks of
his touch.

"Come back here after Greece?"

"Yes, an inhabitant of the Left Coast.
What about you?"

"Same."

Carson watches Morgan as she swirls
the remains of her coffee. One of the
guys working behind the counter stops in

front of them, saying to Morgan, "*¿Un poco más cafe?*"

"*Sí, gracias*," Morgan answers for both of them, and he fills their glasses half full with coffee from the Chemex, taking it from its place on a hot plate along the back wall of the work area.

"You talked to Ari and Blanca. You know, about us."

"Yes. I had to. I couldn't find your phone number and asked them to help me look. I had to spill the beans.

"They knew I was upset about losing the number, but they were upset, too.

"They ragged on me for taking a risk with a stranger. What was I thinking? Questions like that. Finally, I told them to drop it, and they did." From somewhere in her purse her phone rings; she fishes it out, looking at the screen.

"Hi."

"Yes and no, but come anyway."

"Right: College and Ashby. I'll be outside."

"Yes. Outside. OK. Soon."

Pushing the disconnect button, she drops the phone back in her purse. "My ride is on the way."

Slipping off her stool, she goes over to the cash register. Carson watches her ask one of the men something that has him checking his pockets, and then conferring with his coworker standing behind the espresso machine that has him hurrying him into the kitchen. She returns with a book of matches. She slips back onto the stool. "Your pen, please."

Carson pulls his pen from his backpack and hands it to her.

Flipping the matchbook open, she writes something on the inner cover. "Here."

The matchbook cover is green, white, and red advertising, in Spanish, a taqueria in Manteca. Nodding his agreement to her command, he slips the matchbook in a front pocket of his jeans.

They both look up at the sound of a horn, seeing a silver Odyssey pull around the corner from Ashby to College, stopping in the bus stop zone. "That's for me."

Carson follows her out to the street. "What about coffee Monday, Morgan."

"Yes, let's do it. Ten at Cole's: Know where that is?"

"Yes I do. Ten it is-at Cole's." Then: "Morgan. This is the best day since I've been back."

Morgan chews her lip, running her hand through her hair. *We need to talk*. "Yes. Me too."

"I want this to continue."

"Yes. I do too. We have time."

Carson watches her disappear through the sliding door of the Odyssey. He wanders back to the bar and, inspecting the remains of his coffee, tries to decide if he wants more. He slides the matchbook from his pocket, flipping it open.

Printed neatly at the top is: *Call me…Call me first!* Underneath is: *Morgan*, with her mobile phone number beneath her name.

Chapter Three

Internal Objects

Carson knows that a table on the College side of Coles is the best; it catches the morning sun, and avoids the chilly wind that blows up Sixty-third Street from the Bay. The usual gray overcast has not materialized, and the sun is already warming the outdoor tables. He has taken possession of a small table in front of one of the large windows of the café that looks out onto College. Through the window he watches several women preparing the various coffees behind the counter. The two overstuffed red leather chairs are taken as is the matching sofa and the inside tables. He has learned that a small latte at Coles is a café au lait at Roma and Strada. He waits for Morgan with his small latte-warm because Morgan is late-in front of him. The milk at the top is stained a golden brown from the coffee that was poured through it.

The matchbook with Morgan's message is still in his jeans pocket, left there since he read it after Morgan had left Roma. The exchange of matchbooks seems to be *carte blanche* to pick up from where they left off in Paris. Is it more complicated than it seems? And there is Gloria Belknap….

He hears the sound of a horn and, looking up, sees Morgan in a gold Lexus SUV. She smiles and waves before turning into the Safeway parking lot across from the café.

Morgan finds a space next to the sidewalk and noses in against the back of the now abandoned Union 76 Station. It always takes her longer to get to Berkeley from Stinson than she plans for, and she knows she is almost thirty minutes late for coffee with Carson. Grabbing her purse and locking the car, she dashes across the street to Carson.

Throwing her purse and Levi jacket on the table, she says, "Sorry. I'll buy a goodie to make up for being so late."

Carson watches her hurry into Coles. She is wearing, as she did on Friday, blue jeans, this time, though, the shirt is black with sleeves rolled to just below her elbows. The shirttail hangs below her jeans, the pant legs collapsing over a pair of black leather flats. There are more jewelry today; the stainless steel and gold Brietling watch, a gold necklace, a gold band with diamonds circling it on her right ring finger, and some stacked gold and silver bands on the index finger of her right hand. He wonders about her tardiness, figuring that the minute-to-minute goings on between them is the best way to begin to understand their relationship.

"There." She puts a croissant in front of him. "Peace offering."

"Accepted. By the way, you're the goodie."

"A piece offering, is that it?"

Carson smiles as he nods, and Morgan smiles back. His smile makes her feel good.

His looks, his smile, his mannerism, his intellect all pull her to him. But she can feel the maleness–the testosterone. He has an idea or a desire for them and just assumes it will happen. He is willing to talk, he listens, he is accepting of her thoughts and feelings, he is accommodating, and he is sensitive to her needs and respects them. But…she thinks that he believes that words are less real than action, and that, most likely when she least expects it, he will initiate some action that will have a significant impact on their feelings toward each other. She thinks it is a good idea to see him as an Aikido master, respecting her space but, at the same time, entering it, and using their combined momentum to usher them in a new direction. It makes her curious….

"When I moved here, I thought living at Stinson and working here in Berkeley would be a pleasant combination. You know, getting the most out of the Bay Area. But Stinson is too far away. It's a trek, and I wouldn't have time to do what we're doing today. I think I'm going to rent the Stinson place and move to Berkeley."

"Where do you want to live?"

"I own a house on Tunnel Road that I'm renting that has a studio. I'm going fix up the studio and move there. You?"

"I just closed a deal on a studio on Claremont. I have three patients, and I'm going to take a couple of supervision groups at Wright Institute while the regular supervisors are off somewhere working on a grant. Do you own your place at Stinson, too?"

"A large part of my father's inheritance was real estate."

Morgan runs her hand through her short, dark hair. Her lips part: Does she have more to say? She says nothing.

"The thought crossed my mind the other day at Whole Foods that Ari and Blanca might not approve of me."

"I don't think it's that. Jealous is more like it. When I told them about you they worried that you would take up all my time."

Morgan reaches over and pulling an end off Carson's croissant, and, popping it into her mouth, chews pensively.

"Driving here from Stinson, I thought here we are, two therapists, and we haven't done what we ask the couples we see to do."

"And, that is…."

"Talk about process—you know, the inter-subjective, what's going on between us."

"Our relationship, you mean. I think that processing, as you call it, has been slow to catch up with us. Until now, anyway."

"Meaning?"

"Well, I think Ari and Blanca have raised it for us. How do we fit into each other's lives?"

"Hiding from me?"

Carson immediately knows who it is, and looking up confirms that Gloria Belknap is standing in front of them.

"No. Not at all."

"Who is this?"

"Gloria Belknap, this is Morgan Alar."

Gloria's mouth drops open and she falls into an empty chair at the table next to them. It is the first time Carson has seen Gloria speechless. Regaining her composure, she repositions her chair to have a view of both of them. "Mind if I sit?"

Today she is flowing in blues, purples, mauves, and a subtle and complicated scent of citrus radiates from her.

"Please. Join us. Can I get you something to drink? A mocha?"

Gloria nods, and Carson leaves Morgan alone with her.

"You're Morgan Alar?"

"Yes."

Again Gloria is silent, staring at Morgan. Then, "How do you know Carson?"

"I met him in Paris."

Gloria's head jerks back as if Morgan has slapped her. It is obvious to Morgan that she is totally undone, and trying desperately to get a handle on the situation.

For the first time Gloria seems to acknowledge Morgan's presence by scrutinizing her from head to toe, a long lingering inspection. "Those Armani's?"

"Yes."

Morgan stares at Gloria in silence, waiting for the next salvo of questions.

"You're starting up a practice?"

"Yes."

"Where's your office?"

"I'm temporarily on The Alameda until I can find my own space."

"Are you in Bernie's place?"

"Right. There's an office to rent or lease, and I have it a couple of days a week."

"I see. You've arrived from Europe and are sharing Bernie's office."

Morgan does not like Gloria. Actually she senses that she is dangerous. "It's not exactly like that. I had a seminar from Bernard when he was a guest lecturer at the University of Chicago. But, my main contact with the Lanes is with Blanca.   Actually, she suggested I use the office in Bernard's building."

"Are you and Carson an item?"

"Not really. It's more like we're hanging out, getting to know each other."

"Hanging out. How long?"

"Since Paris."

"So, you're back here, and picking up where you left off."

Morgan is tired of trying for accuracy. "I guess you could say that."

"Are you involved with BAKS?"

"Yes."

Carson is back with Gloria's mocha.

Gloria loses interest in Morgan, turning her attention back to Carson. Her blue eyes are hard and angry even though she is smiling. "Carson: You're a bad boy. You didn't tell me you know Morgan. It's lucky I saw you here with her."

"Sorry. I did tell you I met her in Paris."

"You didn't tell me her name."

"You're right." Carson does not want to continue. He is sure that what he says will have no affect on what she believes.

Gloria has made her point. She takes a sip of her Mocha. "Ugh! Carson this is cold." Before Carson can answer, Gloria looks at her watch. "No matter. I have to go…clients waiting for me."

Turning to Morgan: "Nice to meet you Morgan. I'm really looking forward to being in BAKS. "I'm very interested in BAKS. I think I have a lot to offer such a gathering. It would be very nice for us to be peers dealing with professional and clinical issues together."

Carson sees Gloria blink rapidly as she gathers her purse and stands up. "Well I should leave you two lovebirds to each other. Oh. Morgan. Can I have a business card?"

Morgan digs around in her purse, finally pulling out a silver cardholder.

Gloria inspects the proffered card. "Thanks. Nice. Oh! Are you board certified? I don't see your number on the card."

"I am." Morgan waits, and Carson does, too.

"Like I said Morgan, nice to meet you. Good luck with lover boy. And be careful… he's not always forthcoming."

Morgan and Carson watch her walk down College, past the shops and the Bank of America, and disappear around the corner of Sixty-second Street.

"Just what does that mean?"

"I really have no idea. Honest."

"You're dating her?"

"No, Morgan. I sub-let her office, which has turned out to be a big mistake. She has also been pestering me to go to dinner with her-her treat-but there is no way…."

"Well Carson, that is a woman scorned. She thinks you're dating her."

"Thanks to my stupidity. I had suddenly found myself with a couple of clients and no office. I saw her ad, took a look at her office, and jumped at the opportunity without thinking. Turns out she is very intrusive-brittle, demanding, no boundaries." Carson sighs, pulling on his ear. "I'm afraid I've drawn you into to this, too."

Morgan laughs and then sighs. "Yes…I'm the other woman. She was really caught off guard and didn't like it at all…not at all. Even though she walked right into it, I'm sure her spin on it is that we ambushed her with the intent of one-upping her."

Carson sighs. "Reality has caught up with us."

"For her everything is personal, everything is the other person's fault. She'll carry a grudge."

"Well, I suppose she may well strike again, but let's not live with the anticipation. Folks like Gloria can try to draw you in, but if you obsess about them, you become their slave."

"Well, I don't like her. And…she's rude. She interrupted us."

"She did."

"We were talking about us."

"Ah. Yes, processing."

"Right." Morgan is silent, waiting, her eyebrows arching slightly.

"I didn't go to *la grande danse* to find romance, but…."

"Ba, Ba, Ba, Barbara Ann…."

"Yes: A lovely day and a lovely night of a rockin' and a reelin'."

"And in the morning…?"

"The same as now: hot fires burning and the desire to continue. You?"

"I was curious. Jon had talked about you, and from the very start it was so… special. My radar was working fine, the maps in place, but after the first time we got caught in the doorway I stopped paying attention to them."

"Gravity."

"Yes. Gravity. Of course after you had gone your way and I was with Ari and Blanca, and thanks to them, I felt unsure, and with their urging did some soul-searching. But in the end I stopped listening to them and stopped trashing myself."

"Why?"

"They hadn't been there."

"And then we lost and found each other. And, as I've said, reality has caught up with us."

"But…at the same time… we hardly know each other."

"So far. My sense is that we need to make room in our lives for the other."

"Get to know each other."

"We hang out."

"That's it."

"Well, yes. It seems that we followed gravity in Paris, and there's no sense in changing now."

"I hope gravity and reality aren't oil and vinegar."

"Good point. The halcyon days are over."

Morgan runs her hand through her hair. "Ok. We deal with it."

"What are you up to this evening?"

"Going to Cesar's with Ari and Blanca. Then it's to Bernie's to work on organizing the Kohut group. What's your weekend like?"

"Cade has been making noises about coming to the City, and if he does I'll hang out with him. Otherwise…." He shrugs, "Who knows."

"Call me?"

"For sure," he says. "Walk you to your car."

Just as at their reunion there are the quick kisses, Carson kissing each cheek, Morgan receiving the kisses with pursed lips. For them, this familiar contact smoothes their parting and creates the promise of a future meeting. Then, after buckling her seatbelt, she rolls down the window.

"Carson. You can use the office I'm using."

"I might take you up on that. And… let's keep making time, and space, for each other."

"We didn't let Gloria Belknap ruin our time, didn't let her suck us into her craziness."

"Certainly a good sign," he says. "Now that we're in the real world, we can't let the likes of her derail us."

"Don't forget to call."

"I won't."

Gloria Spreads the Word:

I met the two latest additions to our mental health community the other day (They sure are cute together.) Morgan Alar, M.D., and Carson Arrowsmith, Ph.D.

Dr. Alar said she was board certified in California, but when she gave me her card I was surprised that her certification number wasn't on it. But, never fear, I checked and she is. All's well that ends well.

Chapter Four

Omar Rome

Morning Ritual

Gloria Sends a Message:

Carson. I am shocked and disappointed by your decision to break our contract for use of my office: reprehensible and unconscionable. I thought we were friends. I expect you to continue to pay the fee for the rest of the agreed upon year.

The hot water cascades over Carson soothing his body, battered by three games of handball with a twenty-five year old speedster. He had surprised the young guy with his quickness 15 to 8 in the first game-scoring the last eight points, but, youth had its day and he lost the second two, 10-15 and 10-21. A couple of times he had lost his concentration thinking about Morgan and Gloria-a surprise because of late he had not been immersing himself in reflection, opting instead for the more concrete path of action or, especially *with Morgan,* following the pull of gravity. He thinks his reflection is a reaction to his passivity with Gloria.

Problems. The problems are pilling up. Pensively he shampoos his hair. He increases the hot water, the warmth feeling good on his head. He likes showering in the RSF locker room. It reminds him of his days as a ball player.

He wants to believe that, going in together with Morgan to set up a therapy center, Cafe Simone deB, they are going to call it, in the building she bought within the last two weeks, is the culprit: There is a lot of work to do.

But it's not. Plain and simple it's Gloria, now more than ever, a loose cannon ball. The issue is not her craziness, rather it's the misinformation she is saturating the internet with, salvo after salvo of mass mail addressed to what she refers to as the psychological community. The problem is to get her to stop.

Carson lathers his face. He starts, as he usually does, by drawing the razor down the left side of his face. Although the sensation is light he feels the slight drag on the razor as it contacts and cuts his beard. He overlaps the strokes until the area is clear of shaving cream, finishing by shaving carefully around his mouth, pushing out the area to be shaved with his tongue. He holds his face under the stream of water for the last time and, turning off the water heads, toward his locker. He checks his watch: *Time for coffee with Morgan.*

Carson pushes the locker door closed and leaves the gym, heading towards his car. Pulling his iPhone from his jeans pocket, he calls Morgan.

"Hello."

"Hey, Morgan. It's me, Carson."

"Oh, Carson I have been waiting…. The coffee is on."

"I'm on my way."

"I'm not dressed yet." She hangs up without waiting for him to respond.

Carson turns right off Tunnel Road where the cement barrier ends at the point the difference in elevation between the opposing lanes becomes level. A black Honda Civic that had been following closely continues up Tunnel Road.

Morgan is now in her small, white stucco studio apartment on Tunnel, and as he pulls into the driveway, Carson can look up through large front windows and see the expansive skylights, surrounded by red tile roof. Today the skylights are still covered by their white curtains. On the same property, which extends back from the studio, is a large house, also of white stucco and red tile. Morgan owns the entire property, and rents the larger house to a visiting professor at the University.

He sprints up the stairs to the front door, taking them two at a time. He knocks with the brass knocker, and Morgan, in a beige bathrobe tied tight at her waist, answers almost immediately.

"Hi Carson."

"Hey, Morgan. I hurried. You said you weren't dressed."

She laughs. "Sorry, that was five minutes ago. The coffee is ready." She steps back from the doorway, turning toward him. Her eyebrows arch.

"What?"

"You smell good."

She laughs, "Thanks, it's Peet's Espresso Forté."

"No. You. Sun drenched roses."

"Just teasing. Thanks."

Carson follows her through the large living room that takes up most of the main floor of the studio to the kitchen- a narrow alcove separated from the living room by a wooden-topped counter. On the counter is a coffee press. In it dark liquid is topped by amber foam. Next to it there is a chrome frother full of milk. As Morgan readies the coffee, pouring it into mugs and topping off with foamy milk, Carson notices that she has already applied her make-up, and put on small diamond earrings.

Morgan looks up at Carson, and runs her hand through her hair. "Here. Enjoy the coffee. I'm going to run upstairs and get ready. I won't be long."

"Sit and chat?"

"Don't think so. Got to get dressed- takes some time you know. You go ahead and relax. I'll drink mine while I'm getting ready. OK?"

"OK."

Carson watches her climb the stairs to the balcony hallway that circles the large room below. She disappears into her bedroom, leaving the door ajar.

In her bedroom, Morgan goes into the bathroom puts her coffee down on the tile counter.

Taking off her bathrobe, and carefully slipping it over the hanger on the back of the bathroom door, she heads back into the bedroom to dress. She realizes that she does not have her coffee and goes back to the bathroom to retrieve it.

Morgan has carefully placed her clothes on the bed. She dresses thoughtfully: Long skirt-reversible with the print pattern showing today–a T-shirt with a sweater over it, and a long, sleeveless vest-like sweater. She finishes off with a pair of *Arche* flats, her watch and rings.

Morgan takes a last look in the mirror, gets her coffee, and steps into the hallway. Carson is slouched on one of the sofas, drinking his coffee.

He has wandered from the kitchen into the main living area of the studio, which is furnished sparsely but elegantly. He sits down on one of the two leather sofas. There is another on the other edge of the large Persian rug. A glass-topped table sits in the middle of the rug.

Hanging on the wall, behind a sofa there is an unusual framed work of art. Getting up, he navigates around the sofa, and stands in front of it. He realizes it is actually half a work-of-art; a minimal dark figure done in conti crayon on brown paper.

It appears to have been carefully torn so that it is obviously a sketch of a figure done by Giacometti. He assumes it is Alberto from the style. It is an interesting study, but...*where's the other part*? A mystery he can no doubt solve by asking Morgan. Wandering back to the other sofa, he lets himself fall into it, letting himself relax.

The coffee is good. He enjoys the bitter taste muted by the milk. It is quiet here, and there is time to think.

He stretches his legs and stares up at the door to Morgan's bedroom. Although still ajar, it reveals nothing-no sound, no shadows escape from the sanctuary.

Morgan appears at the doorway of her bedroom, moving to the top of the stairs. She is dressed, and looks ready to leave for the office.

"You look nice." He pats the sofa cushion next to him. "Sit."

"Thanks." She sits next to him, close, so they are touching.

Morgan sighs. "I like our morning coffee together. I like what's happening and all, but I had no idea that it would be so demanding and stressful. And, of course, I never planned on the likes of Gloria Belknap."

"I know what you mean. We were in a bubble in Paris."

"That is so true." Moving away from Carson, she stretches, and rubs the back of her neck. Then leaning back to Carson: "Still having fun, though."

"H'mm. Me, too." Carson pulls on his ear. "We're making space for each other… what we had in Paris is settling in with us here, too."

"In the form of bubbles."

"Lots of them…I hope. Are we still on for dinner?"

"Yes. I'm looking forward: I'll be done around six."

"That's perfect. Where do you want to go?"

Morgan shrugs. "I don't know. Let's decide this evening."

"Fine by me."

Morgan sighs, and then pulls on Carson's ear before checking her watch. "OK. Time to get going." It takes her several minutes to finish getting ready, mostly gathering the coffee cups, putting them in the washer, and checking to see if stove is off, windows locked, and so on. Then she grabs her purse and a slim briefcase from a chair.

"Morgan. What is the history of that print?"

Morgan stops and looks at the fragmentary figure striding across the barren, brown paper landscape, apparently unaware he has lost half of himself. "My father's. I didn't know he had it, but it was mentioned in his will, and I found it stored at the Stinson place."

"Any meaning…significance to it?"

"I don't know. It's obviously half of something else. I had it checked, and it's not an original…more likely a skillful likeness of a Picasso or Giacometti. It has some writing...numbers and some letters grouped together giving the impression that the missing half has them too." She shrugs and then sets the alarm. Outside she closes the door, checking to be sure it is latched, and they hurry down the stairs to Carson's Astro.

The drive to Cafe Simone deB is in silence. Their thoughts, feelings, and images of each other recede into background. Soon there will be files to review, situations

for reflection...the inner worlds and lives
of others to plunge into.

Trenches

Morgan wanders about her office, shak-
en and angry. The day had unfolded in the
usual manner, patients arriving as scheduled, intense conversation, and then ar-
rangements made to meet again the following week. Then Pru arrived at her door, a
worried look on her face. "A young woman
is in the waiting room. Her boyfriend
beat her up."

Seeing Angela so bruised and abused
was shocking. Apparently Angela had run
from her apartment fearing for her life.
Where can she stay? What is going to
happen next? *The asshole!* How can one
person do such a thing to another human
being? She tries to put distance between herself and the anger-tries for a

detached concern. She hears a door opening and, crossing the room, looks into
the hallway. Carson is walking towards
her office.

"What's up?"

Morgan sighs. A new wave of anger
washes over her. Her new found clinical detachment slips away, and again she
is furious-furious that any man would do
such a thing. *I would never allow that to
happen.* When will Angela be able to make
such a shift? What can she do to facili-
tate the transition? She stands a bit
straighter and takes a breath. Letting
Carson's presence be comforting, she runs
her hand through her hair.

"I saw a woman who had been beaten
up by her boyfriend; he gave her a real
going over. The bruises looked awful."

"That's not good. What did you do?"

"I talked to her for a bit, but I realized she was in pain and needed looking
after. I called Marlene, and Pru took
her to the hospital so she could be looked
at. When you came out of your office I

was realizing how angry and upset I was. Angela, that's her name, is afraid of him-Wes is his name. She's backing away from admitting it was a beating. Says she may have done something to cause it."

Carson looks at her. He draws in a breath and slowly lets it out.

"Tough. Dealing with your feelings and with hers at the same time."

When Morgan hears this, she again realizes that her clinical detachment had served as a buffer while she was talking to Angela and her other two patients who followed. Again she lets her feelings come flooding back to her. Now, mixed with the anger, is despair and hopelessness.

She hears Carson say, "Is there anything I can do?"

"No. I have time this afternoon, and I plan on talking with her. I want to get her on firm ground." Phone numbers of shelters, friends, escape plans, things like that, float through her mind. How directive should she be? How strong is Angela? What does she want?

Carson says, "Is she in danger? I mean, is the guy still around? Should you notify the police?"

Carson's question focuses her. She will have to be sure Angela finds a safe place to stay. She will have to assess Angela's ability not to return to Wes-at least for a while.

"Thanks. Good question. When Pru brings her back, I'll check all that out."

"Okay, keep me posted." Morgan runs her fingers through her hair. Pru comes into the hallway.

"We're back. Somewhat of a clean bill of heath and some pills."

Angela appears behind her, looking pale and disoriented.

"Angela! I'm glad your back. Let's talk in my office."

Oh, Angela. You take up so little space. Morgan had watched Angela slip out of her office so quietly, so lightly, that no trace of her remained–somehow she has learned to be invisible…a desperate attempt to protect herself from a danger-ous and uncaring world. Morgan wonders if she has done all she can. Of course that's not the issue: Can enough ever be done to save Angela from the Wes's of the world? She goes to Carson's office.

"Ready?"

"Really! I 'm ready to relax."

"I was thinking of Garibaldi's. We could sit at the bar."

"H'mm. It's so noisy."

"Cafe Rouge?"

"At this hour…too busy; there won't even be space at the bar. Listen I know a small bistro and pub. It's in Emeryville-where the studios and lofts are. It's called *Au Courage*. Downstairs you can get pub food. You know, fish and chips, hamburgers, and the like. Upstairs it's more bistro-moules, pizza, stuff like that. I like the upstairs. We can pre-tend it's Paris."

Carson takes his jacket from a hook on the back of the door. While holding the door open for her he slips on the jacket.

"Au Courage it is."

After Hours

Au Courage is nestled among the warren of live-work spaces that have become so popular in the Bay Area. The façade of the restaurant is in keeping with post-modern venture architecture. However, once inside Carson sees there has been an attempt to create a European ambiance. The atmosphere is upbeat and festive. A waiter sees them enter and, without inquiry, ushers them upstairs. Carson assumes Morgan has become a regular. Once upstairs, he escorts them to a table by one of the several large windows overlooking the street. The small rectangular wooden table is already set for two, and they sit across from each other. The table is cozy and, at the same time, a part of the hubbub of the restaurant.

Another man appears at the table carrying two glasses filled with sherry, pale and viscous, in small tulip shaped glasses. Acting very much the patron, he sets a glass in front of each of them. Tan, with close-cropped grayish hair, he seems to be in his early sixties. Wearing a black suit with black T-shirt, Carson observes that he manages, very smoothly, to give him a quick scrutiny before turning his attention to Morgan. As he turns his head Carson sees a scar running from beneath his ear and disappearing under the neck of his T-shirt. The man's eyes are brown, with a sense of depth, and make Morgan their subject.

"Morgan. Welcome." Morgan proffers her face and he gives her a light kiss on each cheek while she purses her lips while receiving the kisses, but does not kiss him.

"Seth, this is Carson."

Seth offers his hand, and Carson takes it.

"Hey, Seth… ."

"Nice to meet you Carson. Busy day?"

Morgan intervenes, "We've had an extremely action-packed day, and it's time to get beyond it."

Carson adds, "Snag a chair if you have the time."

"Thanks. I have to get back. For some reason we're totally overwhelmed at the moment. Come during the middle of the week so we can fix something special for you. By the way, the *moules* are really very good this evening.

"Nice to see you Morgan. Carson, hope to see you again."

From the second floor level there is a feeling of suspension. Below, the street is a stage, alive with lights and people attending to their tasks. Everything is in motion, but the sound is missing, producing an otherworldly landscape.

Looking up from the menu Carson says, "Let's go with Seth's recommendation and try the mussels."

"Agreed. Split a salad?"

"Good. And something to drink."

"Champagne."

"Bubbles. Good choice. I see *Domaine Chandon Blanc de Noirs* on the menu. Let's get a bottle."

Carson closes his menu, and pulls on his ear.

"Some French Fries. How about a plate of *pommes frites*?"

"Bad for the heart."

"If I order them, you'll have some?"

"You know I will."

Carson looks at Morgan. Sounding stilted, their conversation is an attempt at normalcy. *Starting again*.

When they had talked in his office earlier, she had look frazzled. Now she looks relaxed, pretty, her features softly blurred in the glow of the restaurant's dimmed lighting.

Morgan's mind has quit churning, slowed down enough that she can feel the stress of the events at Café Simone deB shrinking and receding. She has pulled herself from the relationships of others to her own surroundings.

Her relationship with Carson, has taken up residence in her life.

Morgan feels Carson's gaze and returns it. He looks tired, but his smile makes her feel good. It is easier to see his stress than her own, and she realizes that from the very start of Café Simone deB they have been going full tilt.

Morgan returns his smile. She realizes that they both seem to relax when they are with each other. Morgan runs her hand through her hair. "I feel better already."

"Me too. This is the perfect remedy for the kind of day we've, especially what you've, been through."

The sparkling wine arrives, and after the ceremony of popping the cork, the bottle is nestled in a bucket of ice, and two flutes of pale liquid, a stream of bubbles rushing toward its surface, are in front of them. Carson takes his flute and raises it. "Here's to normalcy."

Morgan raises her flute, and their glasses chime as they touch. "I'll take it-even with its drawbacks."

They sit silently for a while. Morgan takes another sip of her champagne. She knows that it will make her lightheaded. Running her hand through her hair, she can feel Carson's leg against hers. She holds her hand out, and he takes it.

She watches Carson tug on the hair over his ear.

She pours them more champagne. "Do you have hopes…what you'd like for us?"

Carson shifts in his chair. "Our horizon is so short, isn't it? Like I said, I want to spend time with you, you know…hang out with you."

"I was thinking plans. Long horizon, I guess."

"Like marriage, babies?"

Morgan laughs. "Well that's a bit extreme at this point, but yes…marriage and babies…expectations for me."

"Nothing like that. You?"

"Nothing like that."

"I'm not going to suggest moving in together."

"Yes. Yes, I wouldn't have thought so."

Morgan leans back, stretching her legs letting them rub against Carson's. Once again she experiences the dual energies of the ebb and flow of their relationship. She is aware that only a small amount of her need for independence has to be sacrificed to allow for an overlap of togetherness between them. *I have more champagne in the fridge at home.*

As if he is reading her mind: "I don't want to get in your way. Your independence… my independence, too, is very important."

They have stopped eating and are leaning toward each other. Carson sighs, and leans back. It is his turn to hold out his hand, and Morgan takes it in hers.

He hasn't been actively aware of it, but as soon as the man leaves his table and approaches theirs, it seems he knows that the stranger has been watching them. Perhaps, more specifically, watching Morgan.

"Excuse me. I know I'm interrupting. But, aren't you Morgan Alvarado?"

Before Morgan can reply, he continues, "Sorry. I'm Omar Rome. I knew your father, Gaston Allard." He pronounces her father's last name by emphasizing both syllables separately, lengthening them. "Your father bought some land I owned in New Mexico-between Santa Fe and Las Vegas. The three of us-and my son-drove from Santa Fe to visit the property."

Omar Rome, Carson guesses, is in his late sixties. He is tall and angular with brown hair that is graying at the temples and hangs loosely over his ears. His dark brown eyes are magnified by his glasses, which are large, and have square, plastic frames. He has a sensuous mouth that Carson believes can become cruel. His gray suit, light blue shirt and black tie give him not so much a business look as the look of a cleric in mufti.

Mention of her father's name shocks Morgan, throwing her life into the past-a door opening into an unused part of her psyche. It is not a pleasant feeling, revealing a jumble in need of cleaning up.

"Yes. I'm Morgan Alar now. And I do remember you." Then, more cautiously, "Your Donnie's father. How's he?"

"I'm sorry to tell you that Donatello is dead."

"That's terrible! I'm so sorry…."

"Yes, it's a tragedy that I have not been able to get over." He does not elaborate.

"But, I'm taking up your time with ah… uh…. "

"Carson. I'm a colleague of hers."

Rome's attention stays with Morgan: "Are you a doctor too? I know your father was."

"Yes."

"Your father was a shrewd man. What I mean is, he was very knowledgeable, very, ah…strategic as a businessman. My dealings with him were most memorable."

It seems to Carson that Rome has practiced what he has said. His mouth closes-clamping shut-stopping more words from tumbling out, perhaps what he really wants to say but can't. He backs away from the table.

"Thank you. I just want to confirm what seemed a family likeness. Meeting you rekindles old memories."

He turns to go, then stops and turns back.

"Do you happen to have a business card, Doctor?"

Carson feels distrustful and protective. "We were just lamenting the fact that we had both left the office in such a hurry that both of us failed to bring cards with us."

For the first time, Rome gives Carson his attention-fleeting, thorough. Cruelty plays about the corners of his mouth.

"Well, no matter. You are no doubt in the phone book. Enjoy the rest of your evening."

"What was that about?"

"He's scary."

"Creepy. Your father knew some strange people."

"My father's professional life was a mystery to me…still is. Rome is wrong. I never went with him on any of his business ventures. It's uncomfortable to think about him now. That's the usual response when I think of him, which is not a lot-mystery…unanswered questions."

Carson can see the tenseness in Morgan, and feels bad for making the comment about her father. He is not sure Morgan wants to venture into this part of her past.

"I do have father daughter memories, and they are all pleasant. He was gone a great deal of the time, but when he was home, there was always time for me. As I got older he was less father and more mentor."

Carson glances over at Rome, and sees that he is paying the bill while a young woman fiddles with a camera.

"I don't think that woman is his daughter."

Turning, Morgan watches the two get up from the table and leave. "No. I think you're right. Besides he only had his son. She's pretty, though."

Turning back to Carson: "My father was a very private man. I know he had expectations for me. He wanted me to have a European point of view-you know, attitude. He wanted me to be well educated, wanted me to be a doctor. He generously supported me in attaining these things. I guess he wanted me to be free of want. He left his properties to me.

"More existentially... ."

She glances at Carson, smiling.

Smiling back, he says, "Now the real story."

"Anyway. I think I developed a resilience that requires autonomy. My strength is my independence."

"That's the way I see it. You've got other qualities, of course."

Morgan smiles, then, looks at Carson, a quizzical look he thinks. She shakes her head, and then uses her fingers to tease up the ends of her hair.

"Enough."

Carson nods.

Morgan checks the bottle.

"Here.   There's a bit of champagne left."

She pours the remaining champagne into their glasses.

Carson finishes the remaining French Fries. "Let's eat here again. This has been very enjoyable. Hats off to Seth-he has created a happy place."

"Not cheap."

"No. This is the Bay Area."

They are done, and the plates are removed from the table. Both order an espresso, and ask for the bill.

The coffees arrive along with the bill.

They both sit back, looking into each other's eyes, smiling.

Morgan breaks the silence. "Split the bill."

Again, there is silence, and both seem to be contemplating what has been said-what is going to be said. Slipping his credit card from his wallet, he puts his credit card on the plate with the bill.

Morgan smiles…says nothing. She lets her head drop back, gazing at the glow of the lights.

"Let's go to my place. I have some champagne in the fridge."

"I'd like that."

They sign their bills and head out of the restaurant. Carson lingers a bit to check the accuracy of the receipts while Morgan finds Seth to say goodbye.

Catching up with Morgan he follows her down the stairs through the bistro part of Au Courage toward the street.

Morgan is puzzled. "I checked with Seth. Our guy, Omar Rome, isn't a regular. First time Seth has seen him."

"Chance meeting?"

"I guess. Let's not let it ruin our evening." She hands him the keys to the Lexus. "You drive."

After turning off the alarm, Morgan presses a light switch and the downstairs is bathed in soft light. Going to the refrigerator, she stares into it, illuminated by the bright light. Closing the door, she looks at him, "I don't really need any more champagne."

Carson has drifted into the living room. "I've had enough."

Morgan comes over to him. "I'm wearing my Paris underwear."

"You are?"

Slowly she removes her clothes, letting them fall about her on the floor.

Morgan is soft and smooth in the shadowy light. Carson kisses her on her lips and then her throat, then between her breasts. He removes the lacey black bra and continues to kiss her.

"Ohhh. That's good."

She feels Carson's lips reach the top of her black lacy underthings, and darts to the stairs. "Time for a hot tub." She scampers up the stairs with Carson in pursuit.

On the deck, Morgan watches Carson undress before she throws the miniscule black lace on the top of his Levis. Throwing their towels by the edge of the tub, they sink into the hot water, bubbles frothing around them.

"Are there lights?"

Morgan raises an arm above the surface and gives a vague wave. "Over there." When she is by herself, the hot swirling current circles around her body soothing and relaxing her. Now, especially watching Carson get out of the pool to turn on the lights and then return, it seems as if the same currents are contriving to excite her…with success…her entire body is aroused.

Carson settles back into the tub across from Morgan. She is completely submerged except for her head, her lips parted, dark eyes staring at him: her hair is plastered to her head. From time to time her breasts breach the surface, her rose-pink nipples firmly erect.

"We don't need to talk, Carson."

She beckons Carson to her, and, pushing away, floats toward him. When he is close enough, her legs emerge from the water and she clamps her feet around the back of his neck. Bending her legs, she draws him to her.

A car door slams. Was it part of his dream? He is awake, listening. Carson raises his head above Morgan's shoulder; the bright blue numbers of her digital clock on the bedside table tell him it's three fifty-three. Dropping his head back, he pulls her closer to him, her hair smelling of chlorine and a dusty rose fragrance brushes his face. They had cuddled like this as they fell asleep, separating to their own sides of the bed, and then back together in the early morning hours. Her back is warm against his chest as are her legs against his. Her bottom is pushed against him and he is nestled in its smooth crevice. Carefully he slides his arm from around her, and rolls onto his back. There are a few sniffles from her and then a sigh, but she still seems to be asleep.

Leaving the warmth of the bed, Carson goes to the glass doors shielding Morgan's bedroom from the deck and slides open a door, going out onto the deck and crossing to the fence. He cannot see the street through the fence, but he hears a car engine start up and then the sound of a car moving down the street.

Carson's absence from her bed awakens Morgan. Listening, she hears him padding around from his side of the bed to the door. Peering from under blanket and comforter, her view horizontal, she first sees his tulip tipped penis, bobbing innocently up and down as he comes back into the room from the deck followed by the cool, moist morning breeze. Although she does not think it is anatomically possible his penis seems thicker in the middle. It looks that way, and feels barrel shaped in her hand. Her ruminations produce a pleasant sensation between her legs. Rolling onto her back, she stretches, and then draws her fingers slowly and lightly across her belly and breasts. They made love surrounded by bubbles, steam, and heat-sometimes immersed, sometimes not. It was like floating-maybe it was like making love in space. After showering they had come inside to go to bed. They were on opposite sides of the bed when Carson, abandoning his characteristic gentleman-ly attitude, grabbed her and wrestled her to the bed where they grappled with each other. Being roughed up had increased her excitement, and it was very good, and they ended up entangled in each other's arms gasping for breath.

As he gets back into bed, she rolls over to him.

Slipping a hand under the sheets, she traces the contour of his penis.

"What were you doing?"

"Thought I heard something…a car out on the street, starting up and driving away."

She snuggles closer to him.

"Morgan."

Morgan sighs, but says nothing. Slowly she draws her leg higher until it is resting on him–her arm falls across his chest. He slides his arm around her shoulders and pulls her to him and for a blink of his sleepy eyes he feels serene, calm, safe. But, staring into the darkness, and listening for…for what he is not sure, Carson feels himself falling to sleep–a worried sleep.

Chapter Five

Adversaries: Real and Assumed

Gloria Sends a Message:

In case you don't already know. Morgan Alar and Carson Arrowsmith have opened their practice. They're calling it Café Simone deB (After Simone de Beauvoir, the French communist). The practice is in a building Dr. Alar purchased on College Avenue near BART.

I hope they have an open house soon so we all can celebrate the start of their practice.

The aromas of coffee and croissants: As soon as Carson returned from the Bread Garden, Morgan poured the hot water into the French Press. Five minutes later they are sitting at the bar that separates the kitchen from the living room. Morgan is in her bathrobe, and has fixed her hair and put on her make-up.

"This is not my usual breakfast."

"Not mine either."

"I usually have Kashi, or something like that."

"Hot Quaker Oats for me."

"You told me, last night, that the sound of a car woke you up."

"It did."

"I've heard that same sound a couple times. I know I'm probably being overly suspicious but on a couple occasions I've seen a car parked across from Simone deB, and then down the street from here. At least I think I have."

"A black car?"

"Yes."

"Honda Accord? Get a look at the driver?"

"Not really. Black watch cap with long straggly red hair."

"Same for me."

"Jesus. You, too?"

"Well, yes and no. That is I think so. A couple of times I think a Black Honda Accord followed me from my place to yours, but I have blown it off as my over-active imagination. But now…yes."

"What's going on? Gloria?"

"Doesn't sound right."

"Omar Rome?"

"Why?"

"My scars. Like I said, Omar Rome and my father were engaged in business together. Rome made it clear that he wanted to start a social relationship with us. I think his motivation was both a desire for social advancement and to provide an opportunity for Donnie to hang out with me.

"My father was not responsive to Rome's efforts, preferring, I'm sure, to keep their contact purely professional. He never offered a clear explanation that he was not interested in a social relationship with him. Rather, he would always put him off with some excuse.

"I think Rome saw through the excuses and rightly assumed my father believed he was better than him-socially superior. It must have made him seethe with anger. Maybe, for a person like Rome, he saw it as disrespect, a blow to his honor. I'm sure Donnie was aware of his father's feelings.

"This more or less swirled about me. I was busy preparing for high school in Switzerland. And, I was very busy with my girlfriends. I thought Donnie was kind of weird, and always brushed him off when he tried to talk to me at school. I'm afraid my friends and I teased him. He had to get the idea that I thought I was too good for him.

"The semester was almost over, and I was going to leave for Switzerland as soon as it ended. One day, before classes started, I was in the school's rotunda with my friends. Donnie approached me–I remember he was smiling, a weird, silly smile. He never said a word. He stopped in front of me. He had a paper cup in his hand. I didn't notice it then, but later I remember seeing smoke coming from the cup. I guess I couldn't believe what I was seeing. I thought it had water in it. The next thing I know he was shaking the cup at me. I expected to be doused with water. Instead this silver thing with a green tail that was on fire flew out at me–a lighted *cherry bomb*. It exploded in mid-air, peppering my face with exploding debris. My face started stinging immediately. For some reason, some of the debris was large enough to cut me. I had to go to emergency and have stitches."

No sooner do Morgan's fingers finish traveling across her scars, than Carson's repeat the motion, and Morgan, eyes closed, absorbs the sensations. The repetition evokes a powerful sense of being understood. Her voice is breathless as she continues.

"That evening Rome and Donnie came to my house. My father would not open the door, and when Rome and Donnie did not leave, he called the police.

"I left for Switzerland soon after, and never returned to New Mexico to live with my parents. I never saw Donnie again, and tonight was the first time I have seen Omar Rome since that night after Donnie tossed the *cherry bomb* at me."

"What happened to Donnie?"

"The school board expelled him. The board would have been more lenient if my father would have agreed, but he would not. I think that in deference to my father, Donnie couldn't get into any private schools, nor would anybody give him a job.

"Later, years later, I ran into an old girlfriend, and she told me Donnie had been shot dead by the Military Police while he was robbing a PX in Germany."

"Is there some crazy vendetta? Revenge transferred from father to daughter."

"Makes sense. I think it's possible that Rome held my father responsible for what happened. Perhaps I have inherited the act of disrespect."

"Which was your father's refusal to talk to Rome the night he came to your house, and his refusal to ask the school to be lenient with Donnie."

Morgan nods her agreement.

Carson shakes his head. "I trust your intuition. But, it does sound diabolical. What's Rome going to do?"

"Well, with Gloria it's death by innuendo."

"And Rome?"

"Crazy making. That's what it is. Rome has upset me…he's got inside my head. Now I'm jumpy."

"If it wasn't for the mystery car, we could shrug and write it off to being jumpy."

"That's bogus. You didn't see the car last night. Who knows what goes on out there in the dark of night. Besides, there are a lot of black Hondas in Berkeley. Maybe I've made you jumpy, too."

Carson is about to ask, "Then why are we jumpy?" but doesn't…Morgan looks too stressed. Instead he nods. "You're right… we're spinning our wheels."

Morgan sighs. "If I'm going to get Omar Rome out of my head I'm going to have to revisit dealing with my father. That's what I have to do. I don't like being jerked around, especially by ghosts."

She slips off the stool. "Let's finish our coffee in the living room."

Carson follows her, and they end up cuddled together on the leather sofa.

"Better."

"Yes. Better." Carson accepts Morgan's problem solving; he can do that and still be vigilant.

Silence hovers around them. Carson knows they must part soon; the lack of normalcy that exists between two indi-viduals who know each other—who have a history-is lacking with them, and will make saying goodbye awkward.

Morgan likes the physical contact…it feels intimate, and smoothes their soon to happen parting.

"I know we're new at this, but when we part I know that whatever we have together will continue even when we're apart."

"Togetherness glue."

"Is that what you call it. H'mm. It's not sticky, but I do feel the bonding."

"More slippery?"

"Definitely wet. So, that said I've got to get going, and so do you." Leaning toward him Morgan purses her lips and they kiss, a lingering kiss that acknowledges their parting and confirms the promise of being together again…soon.

Everything is difficult for Angela, including coming to therapy. However, this was her third meeting in two weeks. Morgan is walking her to the door, engaging in some small talk to help ease her from the intensity of the therapy to street life. *She's confident in here…will she be on her own*?

After an embrace Angela is on her way, and Morgan starts back to her office only to stop and turn back when she hears Angela gasp. Thinking she has fallen Morgan goes to the porch, hearing mewing sounds coming from Angela.

She is standing on the sidewalk, her face ashen. A tall, muscular man with his fists clenched and anger contorting his face is approaching her. *Wes*!

Running down the stairs, Morgan reaches her before Wes does.

"Wes?"

Angela's mouth opens and her lips twitch but there is no sound. Morgan steps in front of Angela. Fear knots her stomach. She does not like what the presence of this man is doing to Angela, and anger begins to boil within her. "You're Wes."

Wes does not respond…Morgan's words seem to have no affect on him. "Angela!" he yells, "Get over here! You have some explaining to do." He steps closer. Angela starts to walk around Morgan, but she restrains her.

"She can't do that. It isn't safe for her to go with you."

"If you know what's good for you, you'll turn right around and make yourself scarce. I mean it."

"I won't. I'm Angela's doctor. She's going to stay with me." Morgan can see the rage on Wes's face. She has to will her knees not to buckle. "If you care about Angela and want to do what's best for her, you're the one who has to become scarce…I mean it."

"I know who you are, bitch!" He bows, and there is a smirk on his face. "Oh, excuse me. Doctor Bitch! You're the one who has been fucking with her head. Trying to split us up. That's not going to happen. No way!" He takes a step toward Morgan.

"Don't do this. It won't make things better."

"You better get your ass out of here while it's in one piece or you'll get the same thing Angela is going to get." There is another mock bow. "Come to think of it what you need Doctor Tight-ass is to know your place." Wes's quickness surprises Morgan...in a single fluid motion he is inches from her, trying to grab her shirt. Morgan raises her arm to fend him off, and he grabs her arm...the pain from his grip, is excruciating.

"Hurts!"

Wes's attack on Morgan galvanizes Angela. She grabs at Wes, pulling on his arm. "You let go of her!" she screams.

"Fuck you!" He flicks Angela away as if she is weightless, tossing her to the ground.

Turning back to Morgan he grabs her, and this time she is unable defend herself. She feels his hands on the front of her shirt. He leans close–she feels his heat. He is close, almost touching–his lips brush against her ear as he whispers, "Bitch! Know what? You need a good fuck!" The reek of sweat and tobacco spill from him onto her. She is repulsed by his closeness. Again he is smirking. She knows what he is going to do. Her hands grab at his wrists, trying to keep him from tearing her shirt open.

"No!" Anger bursts out of her, and she drives a knee up into his groin. For an instant nothing happens, then he gasps… she can feel his spit peppering her face, but at the same time his grip loosens, and she wrenches herself away falling back bouncing against a light pole.

Letting out a scream Morgan charges at Wes, hands, shaped like claws, reaching for his face. "Asshole!" Wes slaps her away like she is a bag of feathers, leaving her head buzzing.

"Police! Back away from her." The words freeze Wes. Walking across the street is a woman in blue jeans with a black leather jacket over a white T-shirt.

Words tumble from Morgan. "This man is threatening my patient. He wants her to go with him, but he's already beaten her once."

The cop looks at Angela who is cowering on the sidewalk, and she nods. Turning to Wes she pulls her leather jacket open, revealing a police shield attached to her belt. "OK, dirt-bag, get the fuck out of here. Now!"

"And what if I don't?" He takes a step toward her. "Bitch!"

It happens so quickly that all Morgan sees is the gun in the cop's hand. She points it at his face and then slowly lowers it until it is pointed at his belt buckle. "One more step and I'll blow your dick off."

Morgan sees fear in Wes's eyes. He seems confused, unsure. Lips twitching he looks from the cop's face to the gun aimed at his crotch. "Cunt!" He turns and walks away.

The cop's nostrils flare, and she raises the gun, aiming at Wes's back. Her face is impassive as she squints down the barrel of the gun that she is now holding in both hands. Then she lowers it and watches Wes walk away, waving a hand at

the back of his head as if he is trying
to fend off something, trying to deflect
something from hitting him. His pace continues to increase and he is almost running when he disappears around the street
corner and is gone.

Morgan finds her voice. "Thank you.
I…."

"…Who are you?"

"Doctor Morgan Alar. I'm a psychiatrist. This woman is my patient."

"I don't like shrinks. Up to no good
most of the time. But, you were doing
pretty well. You were standing up to him.
Pricks like that are cowards. They don't
like it when we fight back.

"My advice to you is to go inside and
call the Oakland Police. Have that jerk
arrested."

Angela's voice is plaintive: "Oh no.
Can't do that. It'll make him mad."

"Listen! If you don't bust that dick-
head he'll come after you until he has
his way with you. Then, to Morgan: "Take
your wimpy patient inside and call the

police. He had his hands on you. He assaulted you. If she won't, you take some responsibility."

Morgan knows she is right. "What's your name, officer?"

"Jessie Ritter. Lieutenant Jessie Ritter, SFPD." Jessie turns and crosses College.

"Jessie Ritter!"

Jessie stops in the middle of the street, and turns, facing Morgan. She waits.

The two women appraise each other. Morgan tries to see within, to gain a sense of the police officer. Jessie observes, looking for information she can use to create a profile of the doctor.

"What would you have done if Wes had tried to grab you?"

Jessie's face is impassive, but her eyes are dark with emotion, emotions that Morgan senses are powerful and in conflict, but cannot fathom.

She nods at Morgan.

Is she telling me I should know, or saying goodbye?

Jessie returns to her car, and without another look, drives away.

Chapter Six

Respite

Sequestering Morgan at her Stinson house was a good idea. Wes seems to have disappeared from the scene, and Gloria has stopped calling and sending e-mails. Still they stayed around the house during the day, and set the alarm at night.

Morgan's Stinson Beach house is at the end of a gravel road a short distance from where the Pantoll grade meets Highway 1. A shallow stairway of railroad ties leads from the parking area to a terrace, facing west, that is protected from the sun by a wooden arbor draped with a canopy-the kind used by nurseries to provide shade. Also leading from the parking lot is a well-worn path to a bench overlooking the village and the Pacific Ocean beyond.

The heart of the rammed earth house is the large kitchen with hallways, one on each side, leading to the bedrooms. The kitchen, more aptly the living area boasts a large wooden table in the middle of the room with the cooking area adjacent to it. There is a fireplace at the other end, an old rug in front of it that is surrounded by a sofa and several comfortable chairs.

The day had been sunny and mild, but at sunset, the temperature dropped bringing with it a heavy dampness. However, the fire has made the kitchen warm and cozy. Morgan and Carson have finished the dishes, and are at the table, glasses of red wine in front of them—a Sancerre Morgan had found at the Star Grocery.

"Did you like today?"

"A lot. I still get jittery now and then…my heart races and my mind ramps up with images of his taking his revenge on me." Morgan thinks about the purple bruises on her chest, and then Angela who is staying with her girlfriend, Carmen. There have been no calls…. "I don't think I'll forget the grossness of Wes's hands on me, his smell. But when I'm calm and can be detached, like now, and think of him, I get mad. I believe all women have the fear that a man will try to hurt them. Some, actually too many, really go through some kind of attack and now I am one of those women. Before Wes I never really worried…Donnie did plant the seed… it can happen. For a woman…for me…violence is always a possibility."

Morgan leaves the table and goes to the sofa, falling into it. Carson follows her, sitting at the opposite end, facing her.

"All women sense the vulnerability. I guess you're saying it's always in the air. I would guess that how a woman reacts has a lot to do with how she deals with the event."

"Yes. That sounds right. It's the old thing of victim versus fighter." Morgan is silent. Then. "That's what I want Angela to learn. I want her to be a fighter. I want her to believe it's insulting to be hassled by a man.

"There's attitude, too. Some women seem to project a certain attitude that keeps men from trying to abuse them.

"But really…what has kept me awake is a worry about Omar Rome. He's a creepy guy. The thing is, though, that when I start worrying about him, it invariably leads to my father. The possibility that he is the crux of something I am now the target of is unsettling to say the least."

"What was he like? What was he like as a father?"

"Gaston Alar. Herr Doktor Gaston Alar. He was Swiss born…Zurich-a physician, but he never practiced. After medical school, he sold the family farm and used the money to start what was to become a very successful international real estate business. He met and married my mother, Maria Alvarado when he was in New Mexico.

"When I was twenty-three he disappeared while he was backpacking alone in the Sierras. No trace of him was ever found."

"What was he doing in the Sierras… that's a long way from Santa Fe."

"He had expanded his business to California…the Los Angeles area. Sometimes he would drive, and on his way back he would stop and spend a few days camping at Lake Tenaya and go backpacking from there.

"Later, thinking about him, it fit…he was a loner, I think. When I was younger I saw him as formal, formal with an aura of mystery woven in. The mysterious part was very subtle, like the hint of fall approaching when it is still summer, or the faint lingering of perfume or coffee in an empty room. Still, it seemed he had secrets that he kept from us, and there were questions I should not ask. My mother was very accepting of him. So I think, modeling after her, I took on the attitude of acceptance also.

"The formality worked for us—it provided a structure where I felt safe being myself, and I felt I could learn from him without feeling it was all about pleasing him.

"We never knew when he would be leaving on a business trip, or when he would return. When he did leave my mother and I heaved a sigh of relief. For me it was jeans and T-shirts, sandals, more jewelry, and hanging out with my friends at the park in Santa Fe. I would sleep with my mom in her bed and go to market with her. We would babble away in Spanish. She would fix Mexican food—plenty of rice and beans. I loved it. Of course when he returned, it was back to skirts and dresses, regular shoes, and no late evenings at the park."

"And no more rice and beans?"

"Right. American food, he would say. When he returned from one of his trips, he would bring me gifts, usually books. But he would also give me pens, notebooks, and nice posters and prints for my room.

When he was home we would talk, go to museums...more than once we drove to Taos to spend the day. He had strong thoughts and beliefs. He never really said as much but I got the feeling I should also have very clear ideas and thoughts. That's the message I got. These discussions, lectures at times, were carried out in English, French, German with timeouts for grammar and diction lessons...and pronunciation... always pronunciation.

"But I liked my time with him. When I was a teen it was always exciting to walk with him with my arm looped through his. I liked the contact, and felt very sophisticated and grown up. Sometimes I could smell the scent of pipe or cigar on my clothes. Very worldly.

"It was on one of these occasions that he told me he wanted me to go to medical school and become a doctor. He said that science was knowledge, and that knowing the mystery of the soma and psyche was power. Being called *doctor* carried with it respect. I didn't think much of it at the time. It was something a father wanted for his daughter, but it didn't resonate with me.

"One day I watched my father remove a fishing hook from a young boy's foot. I was so impressed with his skill and expertise. Even more so, I was mesmerized by the actual removal of the hook…his fingers were both graceful and purposeful…I realized there was a reason for everything he did, and that each particular movement led toward the successful conclusion.

"Later I realized that the entire time he was working on the boy, he was talking to him, talking softly, telling him that he knew it hurt, but that he was going to help him, and that very shortly everything would be better. From that time on, I wanted to be a doctor. Maybe it was his concern, his empathy for the boy that steered me into psychiatry."

"It's hard to get anything from what you have said, that would implicate your father in whatever Omar Rome has cooked up. Unless we're talking jealousy."

"Or, it's what I don't know about my father."

"So, your mother's last name is Alvarado?"

"Yes. Maria Alvarado. Why?"

"Well, I wondered. Omar Rome asked if you were Morgan Alvarado."

Morgan's memory loosens, and bits and parts shift and change before there is a new balance established. Something from the attic is now in the front room. "I took Alar as my last name when my father disappeared…died. Before that I was Morgan Alvarado. Morgan Maria Alvarado. I asked my mother about it once. She said it was my father's idea. Your father's idea, she said, just like that…Your father's idea. That's all she really said, but I could tell she did not like the idea. It was the only time she let on in anyway that she did not agree with something he wanted."

Morgan stretches and sighs.

"Time for bed?"

"Yes. It's time for rounds…then to bed. I want to curl up with you and a good book. OK?"

"OK." By *rounds* Morgan means the nightly ritual of checking to be sure the windows and doors are locked and activating the alarm.

They start with Carson's room and the door at the end of the hallway. Morgan lets Carson lead the way, giving a cursory check of the bathroom and window. Then, it's down the hallway to check the door. Morgan knows her concern…fear…is irrational and that checking will not make her feel any safer. Still, she feels she must do something….

Their *rounds* continue–passing through the kitchen to Morgan's bedroom and then the door at the end of the hallway. Morgan's suitcase is on the unused bed along with some clothes. Her make-up is in the bathroom along with her pajamas, hanging on a hook behind the door.

The routine ends in the entry hall; Morgan activates the alarm. They had agreed when they first arrived that the porch light should not be on at night, so Carson checks to be sure it's off. Then they head to their rooms.

"You closed and locked the gate, didn't you?"

"Yes. While it was still light."

In his room he is quickly in bed, hardly remembering the getting ready part. Faint sounds from the other side of the house drift to him. He is irked. They are being jerked around by the low lifer Wes and the mysterious Omar Rome. He knows that in the case of Wes the threat is real and that with Rome there is the threat of him being a real threat. Still, there is nothing tangible, nothing concrete, and they are wallowing in the murky sea of *what if*. He is most likely being unfair to Morgan, she has cause to be scared… really scared and to be legitimately irrational as a consequence, but he doesn't have to succumb in the same way…he has the luxury, or at least the vantage point, of some degree of detachment. *I am spending too much time being supportive.*

Morgan appears, white cotton pajama bottoms, ending just below her knees, he kids her about her wearing *pedal pushers*, or asks her if she is expecting a flood, and a red tank top. She pulls the covers down and climbs into bed, leaning over on her side to turn on her reading lamp, giving him a nice view of her pajama covered bottom.

Turning back she scoots over next to him. "What?"

"Nothing."

"Not true. But I don't want to know…." She squirms around, fluffing her pillows, and finally settling carefully opens her book to the bookmarked page, slips the bookmark into one of the pages in the back of the book and sighs.

"I like it here."

"Me too."

In their halos of light, the rest of the room is shadows…an unlighted stage, the pair read. The rest of the house is quiet, and from outside there is the occasional night sound. If this would be their total world all would be well. At least for now it is good enough.

Time passes, and finally Morgan reaches over and turns off her light. Carson follows suit, and they scoot down under the covers close to each other in the darkness. He feels the pressure as she rolls onto him. He smells her toothpaste breath.

"It feels very good to have your support and backing with the Wes thing."

"We're a twosome."

"Yes…a twosome."

"Whatever we have done is because we wanted it, and whatever we will do is because we want to. We are a couple because of our choices."

There is a silence. Carson slips his hand under her pajama top and rubs her back.

"When I was in Paris alone, it was my first trip there, I was having dinner at a very nice restaurant, and struck up a conversation with the couple sitting next to me. They were in their late seventies, maybe early eighties–both pediatricians… retired, spending their annual month in Paris.

"When the woman chided me for being alone…alone in Paris for that matter, I told her that at the time it was so, but that I envisioned many more trips to Paris, and was sure things could well be different if we were to meet again at this very restaurant.

"At this point the man, very natty in a dark suit, light blue shirt with an expensive looking tie, launched into a mini-lecture. He started with; When you leave here you leave alone. We–he gestured to his partner–will leave together.

"He said, We will be walking as a couple, arm in arm, giving us a feeling of familiarity and intimacy….a balance of comfort and relaxation that can't be experienced alone. You know, he said, you can let your hair down, be more yourself, and not be worried about being judged.

"The woman jumped in here. And a couple can spend the night together. There's nothing like being tangled up in crisp white sheets in a Parisian hotel room, she said. They glanced at each other before he turned his attention back to me. In that instant I was bowled over by the intensity of that look. Here were two people apparently defying the common notions of the ages and stages of both individuals and relationships.

"Back to the mini-lecture. Except for the sleeping together, every couple that has a good connection can enjoy the benefits of belongingness–to some extent, anyway. Sexual intimacy is yet another level. It intensifies everything that flows between two people.

"Then he finished up by saying something like, Couples can deal more effectively with the rough edges resulting from the vagaries of being in a difficult situation better than one person alone in the same situation. They can fall back on each other when things are out of joint."

Morgan rolls off Carson onto her back. Using a foot she searches out Carson, and nestles the foot under his leg. "He gives you a lecture on relationship, and yet as you were telling me the story, I got a definite sense of both of them as individuals."

"Same for me. By the way, when they left the restaurant, they were arm in arm."

Morgan has been thinking that talking about her father revealed a legacy from him regarding relationships, or at least some guidelines for her. Carson seems to have countered by implying that theirs is a result of choice. Choice period?

Carson hears Morgan rustling around, and then smells the toothpaste again.

"Kiss?"

"Yes."

After the goodnight kiss Morgan rolls onto her side. Carson follows, looping an arm around her, pulling her against him.

In no time, Morgan is asleep; twitches
vibrate against him as her body relaxes.
Later there will be small, what he calls,
snortlets, occasional soft snorts often
interspersed with soft sighs.

Drifting toward his own sleep, his sense
of contentment is eroded by a feeling of
apprehension connected to the thought,
false positive. Hiding out for the weekend at Stinson Beach had given them a
sense of security, and he had relaxed and
could tell that Morgan had too. Still…is
the security suspect…is it a false security? Wesley Donovan? He is a threat?
Most likely, but Carson believes he will
run if they go after him.

It is Omar Rome that worries him. He
has to believe that their meeting at the
restaurant was orchestrated by Rome.
Why? He cannot dismiss the thought that
Rome wanted to be sure he had found the
right Morgan. Is Morgan Alar the Morgan
Alvarado he has been searching for?

*I will never sleep if I keep this
up.* In the dark, strange house with its

myriad sounds of unknown origin it would be easy to slip down the bottomless well of missed opportunities, guilt, embarrassments, regrets, fears, and shortcomings until the unconscious selected one to release into sleepy awareness. Then, with the possibility of sleep gone and a cold sweat building, it would be laying, wide-eyed, in the dark in the clutch of an unrelenting demon.

No way. Carson slips his arm from around Morgan and rolls over to his side of the bed, slipping a leg from under the covers, seeking the coolness of the room. *Tomorrow we play. Then, Monday, back in Berkeley, in the light of day, we'll put Wesley Donovan out of business.* Carson's psyche does not bid his unconscious to offer him Omar Rome, and with dreams of a day on the beach with Morgan Carson falls asleep.

Chapter Seven

Beleaguered

If the *shoji* screen at the end of his bed were not blocking him, Carson would see the darkness of early morning through the windows facing Claremont. It is quiet on the street; the first bus of the day will not stop at the corner for another two hours. No cars pass by, and there has not been the hollow slap of shoes on sidewalk of the occasional early jogger. He had not awakened when Morgan slipped from the bed. It was the sound of her shower that pulled him from sleep. He looks at her side; the sheets are rumpled, the blankets pulled back and the pillows exiled to the end of the bed-so different from the fluffed pillows behind his back and the sheets pulled carefully to his waist and smoothed.

All his worry about false positives has flown from his head. Yesterday, when they were packing and getting ready to leave Stinson, Morgan's lawyer, Marc Sinclair, had called with the news that Wes had been arrested and was in jail in Phoenix, the result of getting into a fight and stabbing the person he was fighting with. Marc also supported the idea of Morgan's filing assault charges along with a civil suit; it would be easy to serve Wes, and it might, Sinclair thought, keep him out of California.

The news turned their trip back to Berkeley and the rest of the day into a lightness and sense of well being buoyed up by happiness that they had not experienced in a long time. As soon as they each saw their last patient, nine in the evening, they hurried to César's and celebrated, getting back to Carson's late full of food and wine. They fell into bed, falling asleep immediately.

Carson hears the whoosh of coffee being expressed from the other side of the screen. Morgan gave him an Italian *Bialetti Mocha Express* espresso maker for a house warming gift, promising to bring him coffee in bed their first night in his new studio digs. He hears the hum of the microwave; soon Morgan will appear around the screen with their coffee.

After her shower she had quickly dried her hair and applied a bit of makeup before hanging her clothes for the day over a chair in the dining area. It is very quiet outside, as well as dark, and she is the only one inside making any noise-the only illumination comes from the light seeping out of the half open door of the bathroom.

There is a whooshing from the espresso maker, then a gurgling as the pressure pushes the brew into the top of the machine. Morgan likes puttering in the small kitchen, even in the semi-darkness. She likes making the coffee for them while Carson, maybe still asleep, is in bed behind the screen. Best of all, the goings on around her no longer have sharp edges warning of possible danger.

When he had found her at Whole Foods, the first thought to come to her mind was whether she had been saved or ruined. There had been no answer then. Nor was there time for it later during the days when they struggled with the threat to her life and safety. Now, she does not feel the need to answer the question. Rather, she just wants to revel…in being alive…in being with Carson.

Morgan pours the espresso into the mugs of heated milk, creating a homemade *café au lait* similar to what they order at Roma or Strada. At Coles it's a *Latte*. She grabs her bathrobe from the sofa, and after putting it on takes the mugs from the counter and slips behind the screen.

"Coffee."

After putting Carson's coffee on his nightstand, she slides between the end of the bed and the screen to her side of the bed and slips in beside him. When Carson sees Morgan he grabs her pillows and, after fluffing them, piles them against the headboard.

Morgan takes a sip of her coffee. "Whew! That's hot!"

"Thanks. This is great."

"Fun."

"It could become a habit…."

"No. I didn't mean that. I mean that I feel normal; I can enjoy whatever I'm doing without being hyper vigilant. I hate to use the word, but I feel normal. My life seems normal again."

They both slide themselves closer to each other until they are touching.

"So I guess you can relax and enjoy…."

"I'm back from exile."

"Yes. We can let the draw bridge down and let the world in."

"It's a new world too."

Morgan is wrapped in a rose-colored cotton velour bathrobe. Carson thinks she has nothing on underneath it. He slips his hand under the soft material, cupping her breast. Morgan likes his touch and lies still while he caresses her. Then, after taking Carson's coffee from him and putting it with hers on the nightstand, she kneels beside him. Carson pulls open Morgan's robe and she can feel both the coolness of the air and the warmth of his hands on her. She lets him slip off the robe.

Pushing his hand away, she pulls the sheet from Carson, loosens the drawstring of his PJ bottoms and pulls them below his hips.

"Oh! Carson...did I make the coffee too strong?"

"I do feel some pressure."

Bending down she kisses his stomach before straddling him. He feels her fingers on him, lowering herself onto him.

Time is liquid until Morgan slides off, curling up next to him, her head on his chest.

Carson is awakened as the first bus of the day passes the studio. His pajama bottoms are down around knees. Morgan is still sleeping. He kisses her on the head, and closing his eyes, he drifts back sleep.

Gradually, with a lazy willingness, Morgan ascends to wakefulness-there is a modicum of resistance, the sleep was delicious. Lifting her head from his chest, she stares at Carson. His eyes flutter, opening briefly before closing; there is a somnambulant smile on his lips. The reddish morning stubble reminds her of its heating her up when it scratched over her skin.

Warm and cozy and feeling light and free, Morgan believes there has been a change in the direction of her life; a change in direction filled with possibility. She can still feel Carson's presence in her, knowing it will soon fade to memory, joining her other memories of their short and intense relationship. A short intense relationship that she believes is resilient.

"Morgan. Morgan, it's past seven fifteen."

Paying no attention: "Morning…what a luxury…being so relaxed and so happy."

"My matchbook lover." He purses his lips and she kisses them–the second unhurried good morning kiss of the day.

Pulling away, her face still close, breath smelling of coffee: "You light me up."

She rolls off him, slipping to her side next to him. She lets the sheet slide from her, reveling her breast, and then pulls it back over her. "I have my life back. One thing for sure…we're resilient."

Morgan rolls onto her back, and stares at the ceiling. "Lovers and best friends…getting our lives back… now on our terms."

Morgan sighs. "And, if I had my way–we would just continue as we are."

Carson feels an inner nod of agreement. *Same wave length*. "My thoughts, exactly. There is passion, there is caring, and there is, as you have said, resilience. Expectations seem absent, at least not talked about. Most likely decisions will be personal and then brought to the relationship; there will always be a part that is unknown to the other." He feels the warmth of her body next to his….so real. Carson slips his hand under the covers, and draws his fingers along her hip.

She loves his fingers, his hands on her. She wants to linger, but instead she slips out of bed and scurries around the screen. "Whoa! Morning love…can we do that again?"

"When is your first patient?"

Morgan, dressed in Armani jeans and a black silk shirt, reappears, bends down and gives him a kiss.

"Can we do that again…sometime…I mean. Gotta do my hair, fix my face."

She is in the bathroom, and then rushes past him. "Gotta go. Lunch?"

"When?"

"One o'clock. Bye."

Carson hears the door open, then shut, punctuating her departure.

Gloria Sends a Message:

Subject: Heroine or Impaired

Quite a dust-up. It seems the husband or boyfriend of one of Morgan's patients threatened her and Morgan came to the rescue, getting roughed up for her effort. Luckily an off duty police officer saw what was going on, and intervened, sending the bad guy running. I'm sure we are supportive of Morgan after this traumatic experience, and hope that she will be all right. We also hope, I'm sure, that the difficult work with battered women isn't impairing Morgan's judgment…I don't think it has.

Gloria's e-mail dulls the luster of the day. After a shower and shave, he walks down

Claremont to College, stopping in to check things at Café Simone deB before ending up at a table on the street at Peaberry's, a cappuccino in front of him. He waits until it is ten minutes before the hour, and then, using his iPhone, sends a one-word text message to Gloria: Peaberry's.

Five minutes pass before Gloria, having cut through the Pasta Shop sits down next to him. "You can get me a mocha with whipped cream."

While Carson is standing in line he watches Gloria who is busy writing in a leather-bound notebook. Today she is greens, purples, and browns with enough of the buttons of her purple silk blouse unused to show off a beige camisole. In her e-mail she had used the term impaired to refer to Morgan's leaving her office to protect Angela, a code word in the profession to describe a mental health worker who because of personal issues is unable to make clinical decisions that are in the best interests of the patient. For Carson, the irony is that

Gloria's use of her e-mails to assassinate Morgan's character is evidence that it is Gloria who is impaired.

Gloria gives him a big smile when he returns with her mocha, putting it in front of her. "It's so nice of you to invite me to coffee."

"Yes, a *tête á tête* over coffee is nice. But, I do have an ulterior motive."

Gloria frowns and purses her lips, but says nothing.

"Actually, I have a favor. I would like you to stop sending mass e-mails about Morgan and me."

"What's wrong with my e-mails?"

"Well…they're double-edged…double-edged swords."

"What's that supposed to mean?"

"It's not my job to interpret your e-mails to you."

Gloria is silent. She puts her spoon in the mocha and slowly stirs it. Carson can see the cocoa that had settled in the bottom of the glass swirling up and blending with the coffee. "Are you Morgan's messenger?"

"No. I read the e-mail after she left for Café Simone deB."

Again Gloria is pensive, watching him in silence. A flush has crept onto her cheeks and throat, a warning to Carson that the situation has become delicate because she is on edge.

"Are you and Morgan living together?"

"This is the problem, exactly. I can't really share things like that with you when in a day or so I might very well see it in one of your e-mails only with a zinger attached to it."

Gloria smiles and then frowns, and Carson thinks that he has been given a victory by talking to her about the e-mails, but, at the same time has upset her because of what he has said. But when she tosses her head, making her hair fly and then settle back, framing her face her eyes have changed, giving the impression that she is looking through him—he is sitting across from her, but he is not really the object of her focus.

"Morgan's a thief." It is almost as if she is talking to herself…as if he is hearing her thoughts.

"What's that supposed to mean?"

"Well, duh, Carson. She takes things."

"Gloria."

"You should be able to fill in the spaces by yourself, but I'll give a nudge. Like she stole a place when she got into medical school."

"Gloria…that's an absolute stretch. How can you possibly say that?"

"She's privileged and entitled."

"Listen. We're sitting here at ten o'clock having a coffee. We're privileged, too. What's…."

"You're wrong Carson. You're wrong about me. I've had to struggle for everything. I've earned everything I have and that I am. And, I've never had the luxury of having someone pay my way, and I certainly can't claim any special entitlements that will open doors for me. And another thing Carson: I'm sure Morgan is going to steal from me again."

I'm letting myself be sucked into the whirlpool…her vortex of craziness. Carson leans toward Gloria. "Listen. I'm sorry you feel this way. Honestly, I have no intentions of doing anything to hurt your feelings or bad mouth your achievements. I'm only asking you, as a favor, not to write about Morgan or me any more."

Gloria's face changes, softening from a piercing and intense glare to a smile-her face beaming with friendliness. She puts her hand on his, patting it, but letting it continue to rest on his. Carson would like to take his hand away but he doesn't; he knows that while she is trying to influence him to see things her way, she is also trying to maintain her inner-balance-she probably realizes that she has been thinking out loud.

"Look. I'm sorry you misunderstood my e-mails. You know how therapists are; they just want to be helpful. When I first met you, Carson, I thought you were a pretty neat guy. We were gong to share my office…we were trying to set-up a dinner together.

"I guess I got miffed, a sense of dignity thing, and overreacted a bit when Morgan came on the scene. She had the temerity to barge right in. I thought things were good before. I think she has completely hoodwinked you." Taking her hand off of his, she sits back and watches him.

Carson thinks she is afraid her last statement was too revealing. *Grand theft. She stole you from me.*

Before he can say anything Gloria sighs, with enough gusto that a few people glance in their direction, and puts her purse on the table, and then puts her planner in it. "You do understand what I am saying, don't you."

"I take what you say seriously. Your view of things is not the same as mine, but I'm sure we'd both agree that things got off on the wrong foot."

"You mean, off to a bad start?"

"Yes."

"So…what does that mean?"

"That we can't set the clock back, but if you stop writing about Morgan and me in your e-mails, it will take a lot of pressure off what happens from now on."

"So it's all me."

"I'm not saying that. The pressure is the issue, and it comes in the form of e-mails from you that are about us."

"We can be friends?"

"I want the pressure off so that what-ever happens is free to happen naturally."

Carson knows Gloria is well aware he is being stubborn and evasive, and he is sure it is ruffling her feathers…he expects an angry outburst, but it doesn't happen.

She stands, and Carson does likewise. "Tell you what. I'll think about your offer. I was being honest when I told you I've always had to fight for every thing in my lie. To me this is the same thing…again…and it feels uphill to me. Anyway. Give me some time…then we will talk again."

She slips around the table. "Hug?" There is no time to answer. He feels her purse slap against his hip as her arms circle him, pressing her body against his. Her breasts radiate a heat that is laden with a sweet, delicate floral scent. He realizes he has put his arms around her so he gives her a halfhearted hug.

Gloria's laugh is shrill and loud. "Oh my! I've always liked hugs much better than that kissy, kissy stuff the Europeans do."

"She's obsessed with you. And, I'm the thief that stole you from her."

The lunch crowd at Zachary's is gone, and, after each of them orders a slice of cheese pizza and a Coke, they settle on stools at the counter looking out onto College Avenue.

"I often have my lunch here. While I'm eating I stare across the street at the luggage store, and plan future trips to France."

"Ah, yes." Morgan searches across the street, finding the luggage store.

"You know, I approached Gloria like I would with a patient with a very weak sense of self…one whose dealings in the world are based on that fragile self more than real-time interactions. I tried my best to be clear and direct…no accusations, no threats, no getting sucked into her issues. Now, I wonder…you're telling me it's an obsession thing."

"You had to call her on her shit. I agree about the fragile self and all that, but we're not her therapists. Maybe obsession is too abstract. My point is that I think she's a woman scorned and her way of dealing with it is to discredit you, her love object, and me, the thief."

Carson nods, cutting a piece of pizza. "And what better way than to broadcast her crap to our peers."

"I think so. It's possible you cut her off at the pass."

"I hope it's that simple. Obsessed or not, she seems very tenacious."

"I think that she needs you to like her; you gave her a dilemma."

"Hope you're right. We're going to have to wait and see."

Morgan laughs. "I don't think I've ever seen someone cutting their pizza into bite size pieces."

"Lasts longer. Besides the one thing I hate is taking a hot piece of pizza and burning my mouth, especially that little flap of skin behind my front teeth."

"Only in Berkeley! The politics of pizza."

Carson gazes at the luggage store. In front of it, a woman has just finished securing her children in the backseat of her SUV. No sooner has she pulled out from the space, than another car pulls in.

Carson watches the man get out of the car, and stand in front of the store, recognizing him as Omar Rome. He remembers the sensitive mouth with the hint of cruelty, and the appearance of the priest.

A man walks out of the *Los Palmas Taqueria,* carrying a take-out bag, and walks up to Rome-the two men nod without shaking hands. He seems familiar; Carson thinks he was next to the table Rome returned to after he checked out Morgan. He had been partly obscured by the woman with the camera. The two seem to be waiting. Rome watches the other man remove a cigarette box from his jacket and light a small thin cigar.

"Morgan. Look: Over there, in front of the luggage store. Is that Omar Rome?"

"It is. Shit! It is."

Carson's mind is racing, and putting on the brakes he makes it skid to a stop. "Ok. Play along with me. Pretend I'm showing you how to take a photo with my iPhone."

Moran nods. "Close-ups. Get close-ups."

Slipping his iPhone from his pocket, Carson activates the camera function, and leans closer to Morgan as if he is showing her how the mobile works.

Carson locates each man in the small screen, maximizes the telescopic function, and takes several photos of each. For an instant his view is blocked as a Cadillac *Escalade* moves slowly in front of them and pulls into the red zone in front of Zachary's, and then backs into a parking place. A man alights from the SUV and, crosses the street.

Morgan's body tenses as she realizes that she is watching Victor Perdu, no more than a sidewalk's width away. The craziness of the tortured hour they spent in her office, and her struggle to establish some coherence to their interaction-that failed-returns…a combination of a sense of failure and of danger.

"Quick! Hurry. Get his picture! That guy there…by the black SUV."

Carson scrambles to get a few quick photos as the newcomer crosses the street and joins the two men. He is in his late thirties, Carson guesses. His blond shoulder length hair is swept directly back from his forehead. The only signs of greeting are nods of the head when he joins the group. They talk as the newcomer rolls a cigarette and lights it.

The man with the cigar indicates his smoke is out and the new arrival hands him his book of matches. After lighting the cigar, the man offers the matches back, but is waved off, and, instead slips them in his coat pocket. Carson takes several photos of him and several of the threesome.

The two smokers toss their smokes into the gutter, and abruptly turn away from each other. Rome and the man driving the *Escalade* get into their cars while the third man strolls down College toward the BART Station. Carson quickly tries to get close-up of the license plates.

"Carson! That's Victor Perdu! I can't believe it."

"Victor Perdu?"

"Did you get his picture?"

"Got him. Who is Victor Perdu?"

"I saw him once. It was a terrible session-he spent the entire time trying to take control. He came across as very disturbed. He had insisted on a late evening appointment, and when I tried to get him to agree to another session, he would only agree if it was another late evening. He was a no show, and this is the first time I've seen him since that first and only session. He's creepy. Seeing him with Omar is very nervous making."

It is nervous making for Carson, too. The only obvious factor in common seems to be Morgan. What is Rome up to? Who is Victor Perdu, and what is his role in this? And, who is the third man? It is difficult not to conclude that Morgan is the center-point. *Those guys are up to no good*.

Grabbing her purse, Morgan slips off her perch on the stool. "My circuits are fried. Let's get out of here."

Outside, the bright, sunny day does not seem so pleasant, and the sidewalks, filled with shoppers, school kids, and the usual slice of the Berkeley, Oakland scene, do not seem safe. They hurry back

to Café Simone deB, seeking refuge in the
waiting room.

Pulling into her driveway, Morgan looks
up through large front windows and sees
the expansive skylights, surrounded by a
red tile roof.

Nervous and jittery from seeing Rome
and Viktor, she had found it impossible
to engage with her patients. Images of
the session with Viktor Perdu had forced
her from the present into the evening of
the disastrous session with him. She had
decided it would be a good idea to cancel
her remaining appointments. On the way
to tell Pru, the secretary, she remembered that her house had been cleaned,
and that she needed to go and reset the
alarm. She decided to stop at the Star
Grocery and do some shopping before going to her place to set the alarm and
then return to Café Simone deB to cancel

the rest of the day and check in with Carson.

Morgan goes up the red tile steps to the door, and slips the key into the lock. *This is weird*. The key is hard to turn, and Morgan has to work it in order to open the door, wondering if the couple that cleans had somehow jammed it.

She shuts the door and then, carefully, pulls the chain across the door and slips the dead bolt-it works hard, making a rasping noise.

White muslin curtains cover slanted skylights, and in the twilight shadows there a sense of anticipation as Morgan's eyes adjust.

What? Fear clutches at Morgan. Her Giacometti sketch is in a heap of glass shards and broken pieces of wooden frame on the stairs. Looking at the wall she sees a rip in the plaster where the hook holding the sketch had been. The hook and its nail are now part of the debris on the stairs.

Morgan picks up the faint but recognizable smell of tobacco. Her gasp of fear is choked off abruptly as her hands fly to her throat as if to ward off fingers that have clamped down on it.

From deep inside her primal instincts send their imperatives, and Morgan feels her body becoming taut, impenetrable, hyper vigilant. Her attacker is unknown and unseen; fear explodes throughout every fiber of her body, paralyzing her and forcing her to press her back against the door with all her might.

She rasps out, "Please…don't hurt me!"

There is no response to her plea, and in the silence she can hear the mewing gasps of her breathing. Trying to calm herself, she struggles to control her ragged breathing. Finally, after what seems an eternity, she does, and there is only silence.

She carefully and quietly releases the chain, and then attempts to slide the dead bolt. Hopelessly jammed, it will not budge. *Call Carson…Call the police*. She realizes she has left her mobile in her SUV, and feels the panic returning, sweat encasing her body with a film of fear. Swallowing rapidly, she tries to fight off the fear that is again grabbing at her.

Quietly she goes to the phone in the kitchen, finding it missing from its cradle.

Sliding open a drawer, she takes a paring knife from the wooden holder-one with narrow point and sharp edge. *OK...OK. So be it. I'm on my own.*

"Viktor? Viktor! I know it's you!"

Walking carefully around the debris of the Giacometti, knife in front of her, she climbs the stairs. Stopping in the doorway of her bedroom, she can see the curtain in front of the opening to the deck billowing ominously, and the light from the bathroom, the door halfway open, is on. Knife at the ready, she approaches the bathroom, and, using the point of the knife, carefully pushes the door open-it is empty, but there is a shadow behind the shower curtain, tall and narrow, stark still.

"Viktor. Come out of there!" There is no response. Morgan uses the knife to slide open the curtain, ready for a fight. It too is empty except for a towel on a hook.

She knows the chances are that the balcony is empty. But, she must confirm that she is alone. Moving closer, she smells tobacco, the same rank odor she became aware of when she entered the room a few minutes ago-it seems like hours…the same musty odor Viktor gave off during their therapy session.

Holding her breath, she slowly pushes the curtain open. She knows she will see her deck with its familiar objects, but her body tenses in expectation that a man, Viktor, will be standing there ready to leap at her. The deck is deserted, and in juxtaposition to the silence of the room, she can hear a mix of city noises. On the balcony, a dry air swirls about her, playing with her hair. Back in her bedroom, wandering here and there, trying to take stock, she feels a numbness taking hold of her.

"Viktor Perdu! You creep! You are so under my skin."

Leaving the bedroom, she sees what, in her panic, she could not see. The closet door at the end of the balcony is open, and her quick inspection tells her that the three archive boxes she stores there are gone.

Feeling in a dream state, Morgan, almost running, hurries down the stairs, and goes to the front door. Inexplicably, the lock works, offering only a mild rasping complaint as the bolt slips open. She drops to her knees, her head falling against the coolness of the doorknob and she is there in the silence until the mindless fugue lifts. And, then, without looking back, she sets the alarm, slams the door behind her, and runs down the stairs to her car.

"Nothing was messed-up or trashed. But, before he left with what he came for, the archive boxes, he changed things ever so slightly. My underwear drawer left slightly open, my cosmetics rearranged, my birth-control pills taken out of the medicine cabinet and left on the counter, the rumpled bedspread, a dress almost off its hanger…just enough to let me know that he had gone through my things.

"I'm sure he wanted to freak me out, make me cringe, and feel that my privacy and my personal space were his, too. He wanted me to suffer. And, he got what he wanted."

Morgan is at one end of the sofa, and Carson is at the other end, the studio in darkness except for a single glowing candle giving off a Georges de la Tour like illumination around the dinner table. Morgan also knows there are photos of Omar Rome, Viktor Perdu, and an unnamed stranger resting amongst the dinner dishes and wine glasses.

When she got to Carson's, she called him, and then waited with the doors locked and bolted. She hears Carson shift his position.

"So it's Omar and Viktor." Carson rushed back to his studio as fast as he could. He found Morgan jittery and distracted.

"I know Rome. I know the history of our two families. Now he's back in my life. I believe that I am my father's proxy in a vendetta that he had against him, but was unable to revenge before my father died. I have inherited my father's transgression."

"But, it was Donnie who threw the cherry bomb at you. What about that?"

"He'll say I led him on. It just strengthens my position as the candidate for his revenge."

"Viktor? How does he fit into this?"

"I really have no idea. He can't be a hired gun. I feel strongly that he wants me to experience shame and to suffer. Maybe he wants me to feel as he does. I don't know. He's so crazy. I think he's using Rome. But…for the life of me, I can't say why."

When he arrived, Carson took over. He locked the doors and pulled the shades. He even got a baseball bat from the closet and leaned it against the end of the sofa. Convincing her to take a hot bath, he got her pajamas and bathrobe for her from her small stash of clothing, and threw what she had been wearing, still damp with sweat, on top of the washer. There was no talk of going to her place. He cooked her a dinner-leftovers from the *fridge*.

"When I was in the bath you brought me the martini I thought, this is so nice… so perfect…like a prelude to a romantic evening. Then I remembered what had happened to me, and that I had insisted that the bathroom lights stay on, and the door open.

"I worry that all that is going on is going to ruin our relationship."

"It's hardly the time to worry about that."

"Yes. But things are so messed up. This should be a wonderful evening, wonderful and leading to...more wonderful evenings, not me hiding here under siege-cowering over here away from your touch. It's so shitty."

"Shit happens to couples. Ours is happening now. You do remember Paris, don't you?"

"Yes I do. Everything. You know, when I said yes to going to your hotel room, it felt so natural and right, and exciting and romantic, and all that made me feel so good about the yes."

"For me, all the things that we do feel that way to me...feel right and natural. Unless you're completely grossed out about what Viktor did, I'd like you to slide over here...next to me."

Sliding to him, she takes his arm and, when Carson gets the idea he helps wrap it around her shoulders. She leans against him, and he pulls her close to him. She drapes a leg over him.

"Better."

The candle sputters, and then goes out, leaving the room in darkness.

"Poof! That's me, Carson. All of the sudden I can hardly keep my eyes open."

"Time for bed?"

"Yes."

"Listen. Before we go to bed, I want to get back to Viktor and Omar. I have a plan that I want you to sleep on."

"Which is?"

"We force their hand. Go to Santa Fe and you confront him…Omar. We know where he lives, his phone number and all that. You call him, demand a meeting, tell him what you know and that we have proof, and force him out into the open. Their strong suit is secrecy. We'll blow that."

"About what? What do I confront him with?"

"That Donnie's behavior, not what your father did, was the source of disrespect. Your father's actions, rather than being disrespectful, were the justified actions of an offended father."

Morgan, half awake, half asleep, re-members a dry and dusty arroyo on a hot June afternoon. She remembers it as a young girl, and suddenly, sitting in the semi-darkness with Carson, it seems so very important; she is shocked that it has stayed locked in her memory until now. She feels a surge of power as if Carson has just handed her a talisman that will make her victorious in battle.

"Let's go for it, Carson. I think this has a chance. Force them from under their rock…into the light of day. Honor is very important to Omar Rome."

Carson suspects Morgan knows something she has not revealed to him. He has heard the story of Donnie in bits and pieces, and thinks there are more pieces, and that Morgan believes one or more of these pieces will put an end to Rome's threat. She knows something that will defuse his need for revenge.

"Tomorrow. We will plan tomorrow."

"Yes. Tomorrow."

Chapter Eight

Family Matters

Dressed in his outfit of preference-blue dungarees, a light blue cotton work shirt with the sleeves rolled to just below the elbows, and a pair of soft black loafers-Omar Rome leaves the kitchen and enters the front room with its vaulted ceiling and opulent furniture and rugs. He sees that he still has a dishtowel in his hand, and returns to the kitchen, looping it through the handle of the refrigerator. Returning to the living room, he goes to the large window that offers a sweeping view of the high desert of New Mexico. Glancing first at the Pinion trees, some of them dying, he then shifts his gaze to a low rise with a faint path starting on the other side. It is where Viktor's trailer is nestled on the slope, out of view from his vantage point, and connecting to the steps of the large stone covered patio with a fountain in the center that is the entry to the house. Rome sighs.

He sees Viktor Perdu come over the rise, treading cautiously down the middle of the path, looking like he is trying to place each foot in an impression he made the previous trip, and the trip before that, and the one before that. A slight breeze teases his shoulder length hair- straight, blond, parted in the middle- lifting it away from the collar, pulled up to cover his neck, of his white cot- ton shirt tucked into his baggy khakis. Clutched in his hand is his denim jack- et. It seems Viktor knows he is being watched; looking toward the window, he raises his sunglasses with the long deli- cate fingers of his free hand, revealing his dark brown, troubled eyes.

Their eyes meet. Rome nods once to ac- knowledge Viktor who arches his eyebrows in recognition of Rome's presence. Then both men turn away; Rome turns away from the window, disappearing from view as he moves to the interior of the living room, while Viktor drops his head as he trudges across the warm stone entrance to the house.

A click sets off a metallic sound wave when Viktor opens the front door, and enters the front room where Rome is waiting for him, sitting on a large brown leather sofa. Viktor settles in a matching brown leather chair opposite him, and there is silence until Rome breaks it.

"The doctor called me."

Viktor pulls a black leather tobacco pouch halfway from the inside pocket of his jacket before shrugging and letting it slip back. "Called you? Here?"

"Yes."

"How can that be?"

"The doctor said she checked the phone directory."

"What did she want?"

"She knows about you, knows it was you that had the appointment with her. She doesn't know who Mister X. is, but has a photo of him with us. She said she is faxing photos."

Viktor gets up from his chair, and, leaving the front room, slowly climbs the stairs to the second floor of the house. Waiting, Rome idly runs his hand between the leather cushions. Viktor returns, carrying several sheets of paper, carefully placing then in a neat row on the table in front of the sofa.

They are degraded by fax and enlargement, but clear enough: They are photos of Viktor, Rome, and the man Rome referred to as Mister X, and several of the three of them standing together. There are also photos of the license plates of their rental cars. They were taken at the last meeting, the one on College Avenue in Oakland. Whoever took the photos must have been across the street…the pizza restaurant or the hair salon.

"She wants to talk. Said she was coming here. Said it could be her or the police."

"And?"

"I told her I'd meet her in Santa Fe… at the Plaza."

Viktor sighs, and turns to stare out the window. Rome wanders to the fireplace, and then back to the sofa and drops onto it. Viktor sighs again, turning back to the waiting Rome.

"What are you going to say to her?"

"The photos are an invasion of my privacy. That many years ago her father cheated me, and I am still paying for it. She has benefited from this dishonesty, and I want restitution–monetary restitution. I was in the area to see my California lawyer."

Viktor stares at Rome, his eyes blinking slowly; then he shifts his gaze and stares into the large mirror above the fireplace. "Your aura is weak today."

Rome runs a hand through his sparse graying hair, and then placing his hands on his legs, pushes himself up from the sofa. Going to a round wooden table with a highly polished surface, he picks up a

photograph in a plain black wooden frame—
a photo of a young man in a military
uniform with a flag of the United States
in the background. The child-soldier is
staring at the camera, trying to be the
warrior, but the soft eyes and sensuous
mouth of a young boy yet to become a man
blunt the necessary ferociousness. Next
to where the photograph was is a photo of
Viktor, taken many years ago, dressed in
a Boy Scout uniform with a sash of mer-
it badges across his chest and an Eagle
Scout badge pinned to his chest. Like
the photo of the young candidate warrior,
Viktor's face is that of a handsome young
boy, a handsome troubled or worried young
boy. It's the eyes: there is something
in the look that suggests the presence
of something troubling that uneasily reveals itself.

Sighing, Rome returns to the center
of the room, absent-mindedly holding the
photo in his hand. Then, remembering that
it is there and glancing at it.

"I'm tired of this. It has gone on too long. I believe the word is hubris. We are guilty of hubris. Now they know who we are…we are exposed. They are very smart. And they are aggressive, even fearless. The doctor is very much her father's daughter. She does not buckle under pressure. You have failed to intimidate her."

"Perhaps. But, the deed will be done, and when it is, we will return to the protection of the shadows. She will…as you say…buckle." Viktor sits on the padded armrest of the chair.

"To make the sphere whole again, Donatello must be avenged, I must be avenged–you must be avenged. We must complete what Donatello started."

Rome watches him settle on his perch; he does not seem to be paying attention to his surroundings, instead he seems to have gone somewhere else, somewhere only he can go to. Still, he speaks to him.

"Donnie must be avenged. I know. And you. And, God knows, I have waited long enough. Disgrace must be the plan. It is the best. I am convinced its success will settle the accounts."

Viktor rises from his perch, pulling a stiletto from in the inner pocket of his denim jacket, which has been resting on chair's ottoman. It has a pearl handle and a thin narrow, flat blade ending in a sharp point. Viktor runs a thumb and fore-finger down the flat surface of the blade.

"A few drops, a few splashes, will make the sphere whole again, and it will make it pure."

Rome watches Viktor play with the sti-letto, and glances back at the sofa before turning his attention back to Viktor.

"So be it. I will talk to the doctor and allay her concerns. Then we will fin-ish this. But I don't trust Mister X…he is sloppy. Our meeting should have never been so public."

"Do they know who, ah, Mister X is?"

"No."

A smile flickers across Viktor's face. "There you have it…all is safe and well.

He can deliver the potion. Then he's gone."

Rome shrugs, lifting his arms, and then letting them fall back against him. "So be it."

Viktor is still playing with the stiletto; its point cuts an arc through warm, dense atmosphere between the two men. "I am disappointed…in your loss of interest in purity."

Rome's head snaps back as if he has been struck. He steps close to Viktor who holds his ground and for an instant the blade flits back and forth inches from Rome's chest before Victor puts it behind his back. The two stare at each other, and, although he maintains the stare, Viktor's eyes begin to blink rapidly.

"Gaston Allard disgraced my family and me and I will disgrace his kin. That will satisfy me. Donnie will be vindicated. But, my young friend, time is of the essence. The longer this goes on the greater the chance of our exposure."

Viktor takes several steps back, and bows. "I accept the wisdom of your position."

"Tomorrow I will talk to the doctor, and then we will go our separate ways. Everything is in order, I presume."

Viktor grimaces.

Rome sighs. Realizing he still has the photograph of Donnie in his hand, he takes it back to the table and places it in its place next to the photo of Viktor.

"Will you please get rid of that ice pick!"

Looking surprised that it is in his hand, Viktor shuffles to the chair and slips the stiletto into an inside pocket. He then leaves the room, heading to the kitchen. Rome, shaking his head, falls onto the sofa. He gazes out the window, drumming fingers on his denims.

Sounds come from the kitchen, a cupboard door opening, the clink of classes, the refrigerator door opening, and ice clinking. Finally, water running.

Viktor reappears, two glasses of ice water, one carefully balanced in each hand. "I put the hand towel on its hook."

He hands a glass to Rome, then, after draping his jacket on the back of the chair, drops down on it, leaning forward expectantly.

"Thank you, Viktor. Do not be upset. You are very brilliant. You are perfect with details. Sometimes, however, it all stays in your head, and I don't know, in the slightest, what's going on. Just like a minute ago—I don't know if it's that you forget or you just don't pay attention. I'm afraid that, sometimes, you miss the bigger picture."

Viktor nods, looking sheepish.

"I have been abandoned twice; once by my father, once by my mother when my father's desertion killed her. You are my fulcrum that balances."

"Yes…yes I know. Our adversaries are smarter than we thought. And…we have made mistakes. Our final attack must be well thought out and well executed. We go to

Berkeley together, and then, when the deed is done we, ah, disappear; you, on your errands, me on mine."

"Ah, yes." Viktor smiles. My errands in Helvetica."

"And I will be on the Sea of Cortez."

Rome rises from the sofa, moving toward the front door, and his movement galvanizes Viktor, who grabs his jacket and follows him. They both leave the house, walking to the steps at the edge of the stone patio. Stepping from the steps to the faint path, Viktor stops and turns. Reaching into his jacket he pulls out his smoking paraphernalia, and, jacket over his shoulder, rolls a cigarette. Pulling a lighter from his khakis, he lights it–the paper flares for an instant before the tobacco begins to burn. He inhales deeply and then exhales; the plume of blue smoke dissipates rapidly in the soft breeze blowing from the west.

"Omar. We have created an exquisite and complicated web. If you give Morgan Alar any opportunity allowing her to pull or tug any of the strands, she will unravel all our careful work, and we will be doomed. She, granted, is brilliant, but she is also evil-as her father was. Don't believe what she says. Don't placate her. Don't be blinded by her charms. Please don't give into her. She will destroy us if she can. Omar…stand firm, be loyal to our cause."

Each sentence has been punctuated by a drag on the cigarette, and now only a glowing coal remains, which Viktor smothers between thumb and fingers, letting the dregs scatter in the wind.

Rome nods, saying nothing, and retreats back to the house. Reaching the door he turns and watches Viktor, carefully placing one foot after the other on the dusty path until he disappears over the rise.

Born in Santa Fe, Morgan no longer considers it her home. Perhaps, for a while, she missed the dominance of the sky-a brilliant blue canopy stretching to each point on the horizon measured by the compass rose. At fifteen she had left, sent by her father, from the familiarity of the adobe to Switzerland. Before, it seemed that for both her and her mother it was waiting for Europe in the form of her father, her mother's husband, to come to them; returning from one of the many business trips he was always making. Now she carries Europe, blended with America, wherever she goes.

With her back to the entrance of the Inn of the Anasazi, Morgan looks across the intersection of Palace and Washington to the Plaza. She remembers meeting her girlfriends there after school and on the weekends-they always congregated at their special bench across the street from the ice cream shop. Morgan also remembers how mean and cruel they were to some of the boys, including Omar Rome's son Donnie-a strange boy with a strange name…Donatello. Morgan sighs, and then out loud says, "Donnie. This is all about you."

Morgan senses motion behind her, and turns to see Carson leaving the cool darkness of the hotel to join her in the bright afternoon sun. As she did a few minutes ago when she left the hotel, he slips his sunglasses down from his forehead, settling them on his nose. When he reaches her, he pulls on his Giants cap, tugging the visor to the top of his sunglasses. Earphones hang around his neck, disappearing into the pocket of his shirt.

"Our room is ready, and I had our bags sent up."

"That's good, Carson."

"Are we ready for this?"

"I think so." She pats her chest where the tiny microphone is hidden.

Morgan and Carson cross Washington, entering the coolness of the covered walkway of the Palace of the Governors, passing by the artisans with their displays of silver, pottery and weaving. "I feel weird about recording this."

"Well, he's probably doing the same. Anyway, it's good to have a record of what goes on between you two. Lets do a test. Besides, he does any threatening…I want to know."

Carson puts the headphones in his ears while Morgan crosses Palace to the Plaza sitting on the bench agreed upon to be the meeting place. "Can you hear me?"

Carson nods as he continues to the corner, looking across Lincoln at the Museum of Fine Arts before turning to Morgan who is searching the park from her place on the bench.

"I see him. He's coming out of the jewelry store. San Francisco and Washington."

Omar Rome, in blue dungarees, a faded blue shirt, black loafers and a straw hat, crosses the street, and takes the path that will lead him to the bench where Morgan is waiting.

Rome removes his hat as he sits next to Morgan. "Good morning, doctor. I think this will be a waste of time for both of us."

Rome's clear blue eyes stare at her impassively through the large frames of his glasses. Lines from years of worry and stress mar his smooth skin, or as Morgan guesses, it is hate that causes the lines.

"Perhaps. But first, I'm sorry about Donnie."

"You're sorry?"

"Yes. I know my friends and I weren't always nice to him, teasing him and all, but we never wanted anything to happen to him."

"Do you know what happened?"

"One of my girlfriends…from the old days…e-mailed me."

"What did she tell you?"

"That Donnie was shot and killed by MPs, in Germany, during a burglary."

"Thank you for your condolences."

Morgan would like to look in Carson's direction, but does not. She has to take comfort in knowing he is there…close by. She wonders, feeling a chill run down her back, if Viktor is lurking somewhere.

"What's it going to take to stop this?"

"Stop what?"

"Your vendetta against me. I am very sure you believe that my father committed an act of disrespect against you and Donnie many years ago. You hold me accountable for what happened to him. I also suspect that the man calling himself Viktor Perdu has a grievance against me, although I have no idea what it could be since I never knew him until he posed as a patient and we had one meeting. I do know that he is very disturbed."

"You think Viktor is insane?"

"In a manner of speaking, yes. He is also very manipulative. For his own reasons, he has drawn us in to a very sinister situation. We could well be pawns it some grand design he has devised. We could both suffer from his craziness."

Rome sighs. "You are mistaken, doctor, very mistaken. I am sorry about your discomfort. The truth is that your father cheated me. He cheated me and I am still paying for it. And you have benefited from his dishonesty. It is true that your treatment of Donnie was very damaging to me, and eventually…fatal to him. I was deeply hurt by your evilness, but not surprised. After all, you are the daughter of Doctor Gaston Alar."

"When is this going to stop?"

"I wish you no harm. I have considered seeking restitution. But only financial restitution…from you, nothing more."

"Who is Viktor Perdu?"

"A business associate."

"And the other man in the photo?"

"A possible business client. Don't waste your time asking me his name."

Rome is polite, if a bit diffident, and Morgan senses he could be biding his time before making an early departure. She sees the futility in getting Omar to acknowledge the details of his plot, and

the part played by the others. She has
let herself take a wrong turn away from
her intended direction. *This is about
Donnie*.

"Omar, I want to tell you a story."

Rome stares at her, saying nothing.

"This story starts with some rude behavior. I was getting interested in boys.
My girlfriends and I were very aware of
boys. Donnie, we…I…considered him a pip-
squeak. We thought we were very sophisticated, and were aloof to Donnie's attempts, which we thought were weird, to
hang out with us. I remember this one
time when I used my aloofness to rebuff
him, he looked at me with hate, and now
I know, hurt, and said, You think you're
better than me, don't you. Well we'll
see.

"About the time this happened there
was a rumor going around that some of
the boys would follow girls from school
and try to pull down-sometimes pull off-
their jeans or rip off their skirts to

embarrass them. When we heard about this, the victims were usually Native American girls. I never heard that it happened to any white girls, anyway it never happened to any of my friends. I guess Donnie found out about my Indian ancestry.

"One day I was walking home from school, taking a short cut up a deserted, dry arroyo when Donnie and two other boys confronted me. At first they teased me about wearing a skirt, then started trying to pull it up."

She remembers. Both her mother and her father had warned her against using the arroyo as a short cut. However she paid them no attention-what did they know? Besides, her life was perfect: she was an excellent student, she was popular, she felt good about herself, and day after day was a wonderful adventure. Most of time though, she walked with one of her friends. Today she was alone.

"Then Donnie yelled at me, Squaw! Too bad for you: You're going home without that skirt."

Morgan remembers thinking how child-
ish the boys were, while at the same
time feeling vulnerable, which turned to
fear when they told her they wanted her
skirt. At first she could not compre-
hend the implication of what was going
to happen. Then she did: It's going to
happen to me, she thought. The image of
her walking home in her underwear seemed
a fate worse than death. She remembers
the feel of the dry air, cool against
her forehead beading with sweat.

"By this time I had dropped my book
bag and purse, and, even though I was
scared, I told them that there was no
way this was going to happen. I think my
resistance gave Donnie's friends second
thoughts and that Donnie realized this.
He offered that they would settle for my
underwear-Your little panties, he said.
You can take them off yourself, he said.
I knew I couldn't outrun them, and that
fleeing might excite them, so I stood
my ground. Finally Donnie said that at
least I could show them my breasts-titties

he called them. Show us your titties, he said.

"Again I told them, no way was I going to play their silly game. I sensed Donnie's friends had cold feet, and that Donnie would not try anything on his own. I was wrong. When they beat a hasty retreat Donnie stayed."

The image of Donnie circling her is so clear that she feels breathless. He had a smile on his face as if all was in fun. But he had started to breathe hard, and she was afraid he was excited. Morgan remembers his fingers flexing open and closed as he circled her, feigning an occasional lunge at her.

"He lunges at me, and we start to wrestle. At first he's trying to pull my skirt up or off, or trying to pull my shirt down, groping me at every opportunity."

Morgan remembers the embarrassment of rolling on the ground with Donnie, her skirt bunched at her waist, his hands grabbing and pulling at her. Dust, kicked up from their scuffling feet, then hands and bodies, formed a cloud around them, and she could taste the grit in her mouth. She was also in pain from the rocks scraping her hands, her legs, her knees, and, for the first time in her life, the feeling of dread that something very terrible was going to happen to her settled on her.

"Then it got serious. We both begin to hit each other-serious slugging. He was hurting me and I wanted to hurt him back. I ended up sitting on him, hitting him in the face until his nose was bloody, and he started to cry. I knew it was over when he threw an arm over his face and cried out, Stop! Stop!"

Morgan recalls that at a point when the position of her skirt no longer mattered, she realized that she was bigger, faster and stronger than Donnie, and that his efforts to overpower her were inept and ineffectual. At that point the tide turned; she took charge of the fight and started to give him a good beating.

"I unbuckled Donnie's belt, and pulled it through the belt loops and off. I remember holding it over my head."

Morgan also remembers bending down and shouting into Donnie's face, White boy! Scalped by a squaw!

"Did you say anything to him?"

"I told him that I was going to keep the belt, and if he ever gave me any more trouble, I would tell the whole school, using the belt as evidence, that I beat the crap out of him when he tried to pants me."

Rome, for the first time, interrupts. "What did Donnie say?"

"Nothing. He was still crying when he got up and ran away. A week or so later I'm in the rotunda of the school with my girlfriends. I see Donnie out of the corner of my eye, about ten feet away. He has a very funny look on his face. I think he's waving at me and I turn toward him. He tosses a cherry bomb at me, and it explodes in front of me, peppering my face with exploding debris."

Morgan points to the two small scars—one on the bridge of her nose, the other above her lip—thin white lines against her coppery skin.

"You know what happened next."

"Did you tell your father about your… fight…with Donnie?"

"No. I thought I had taken care of it on my own. Actually I didn't tell anybody."

"Why should I believe this story of yours?"

Reaching into her bag, Morgan pulls out a rolled leather belt, and holding it by its silver and turquoise buckle lets it unroll before handing it to Omar Rome. Rome holds it in his lap rubbing the buckle, fingering the leather while turning it over and over. Then he turns to Morgan and nods. "It's Donnie's."

"You keep it, Omar. I think my father thought he was better than you. He thought he was better than most people, but he never talked about it with me. He was a private man; he certainly never talked about his business affairs with my mother or me. I do think he wanted Donnie punished and you embarrassed. He never told me what he wanted to do, but I'm sure he wanted Donnie to be expelled and for you to have your reputation tarnished."

"You give me the belt? Without this, you have no story."

"This is between you and me, Omar. We both understand the importance of truth and honor."

Rome gets up from the bench. "I wish we had never had this conversation. Things will end. But, I fear, not well." He starts to walk away.

"Omar. Who is Viktor Perdu?"

Turning back to her he says, "I am pledged to silence. However, you are a significant part of his life, more than you know, and, because of who you are, he hates you." After walking a distance, Omar Rome turns again. "Hates you."

Morgan watches Rome leave the park, crossing the street, and rounding the corner by the jewelry store, taking the street leading to the cathedral. "He's left the park and headed up San Francisco."

Searching, she sees an SF Giants hat, floating above the crowd, and watches as Carson trades the shade of the Governor's Palace for the growing shadows of the late afternoon sun and heads to her.

It is cool and the light subdued in the small bar tucked away from the brightness and energy of the dinning room at the Inn of the Anasazi. Outside, it will be dusk soon. Carson stretches his legs beneath their table, pushing his back against the leather of the banquette, glancing at Morgan, very pretty in her black Paris dress. After her confrontation with Omar Rome, he had suggested a walk then a coffee at Galisteo News with the hope of giving her the opportunity to talk about the conversation. However, Morgan had remained quiet, and when they got to Galisteo News, neither of them had a desire for coffee. Nor had they an appetite or the urge for dinner in the dining room. So, after a quick change of clothes, they chose the seclusion of the bar.

Morgan feels Carson's nervous squirming next to her. She remembers them wandering the streets of Santa Fe after the contentious encounter with Omar Rome ending with them at the cluttered table in a corner of the bar with a very expensive bottle of Sancerre and sharing some plates from the menu (crab with a velouté of Beets, a tomato salad, asparagus in vinaigrette and Carnaroli risotto.)

"I don't understand Viktor, but with Omar, it goes back so far, it's so historical, and it seems so irrational…it's just so irrational."

"It seems…tribal."

"Yes. Revenge for an ancient transgression of a family member. Payback for an imagined act of disrespect passed down from my father to me."

Morgan pours the last of the Sancerre into their glasses. They had requested an ice bucket, so, to the last drop, the wine is cold, crisp, dry.

"He's lost his humanity. I've been reduced to an object; something that must be dealt with to regain the family honor."

"I think you derailed him. It's going to be very hard for him to continue."

Morgan feels a surge of hope, the first since they decided to confront Omar Rome, but it is quickly squelched by her hopelessness. "What makes you say that?"

"I agree with you. From Omar Rome's point of view the issue is one of honor. I think that what you told him during the conversation derailed him. According to you, in the world of Omar Rome, Donnie disrespected you, and you settled accounts with him. It's going to be difficult for him to continue to see Donnie's actions with the cherry bomb as a result of constant razzing by you and your girlfriends."

"So? What if what you say is true?"

"He will have to pull back. I think he believed what you told him. The look on his face when you gave him Donnie's belt was incredible. I think he's too stuck in his own world view to apologize, but his sense of honor may well keep him from coming after you-it's Donnie that brought dishonor to the family."

"And...Viktor? What about him?"

"I don't think he can act alone. I think he needs Rome to carry out their plans. And, Omar Rome may back away from wanting to carry out their plans. I can see them having quite a confrontation about what was said that, on its own, could put an end to what they want to do. Besides, we've blown their cover-we know who they are. We have photos. They can no longer act in secrecy. We have enough information to connect the dots. We have the recording of your conversation with Omar Rome...."

"God, Carson. I hope you're right."

"At least we may have bought some time. And I believe we have enough information to give to the Berkeley PD that they will have to become very involved and active with their investigation."

The bartender puts a candle on their table.

"Morgan. It's going to be dark soon. Do you want a walk…or should we go to our room?"

Morgan remembers another evening stroll-the one in Paris-full of romance and tension awaiting a very complicated yes or no to complete or carry on the evening. *So different*…she thinks, with a shiver, that her destiny is in someone else's hands.

"Carson…why don't you go up to our room. I need some space. A walk to the Cathedral might do me good."

Carson frowns, "You sure? I mean is this a good idea?"

"That's just it. I will not be a prisoner of those two crazies."

"Ok. See you in the room."

Outside the air is dry and mild. There are still people around the Plaza as they leave the inn, but it is quiet on San Francisco as she heads for the Cathedral.

Before entering, she stops in front of the statue of *La Conquestadora*, feeling the strange wordless emotional tug she always has when standing in front of the statue, glowing white in the late afternoon dusk. As she enters, a woman in her seventies slips past her, on her way out, leaving her alone in the dimly lighted interior, with shadows here and there, cast by the flickering candles. Incense is in the air.

Morgan wanders into a small chapel; there is a bank of candles in front of an altar with a reliquary containing the mannequin of *La Conquestadora* in a white baptism dress. Then turning, she enters the silent nave and sits on one of the benches.

Morgan remembers being dragged here, sitting a couple of pews away while her mother knelt and prayed. She was young, and it was hard to sit, but she finally realized that it meant a lot to her mother, and that her prayers comforted her.

One time in Paris she went into *Notre Dame*, just to take it all in, but ended up lighting two candles-one for her mother, one for her father. She remembers being comforted by lighting the candles and thinking of her parents.

Morgan knows why she wanted visit to the cathedral. She wants comfort and sanctuary. She understands the essence of spirituality and the importance of faith, at the same time knowing that for her there are other ways of facing the challenges thrown at her by Rome and Viktor Perdue. She knows that she cannot rely on Carson for the kind of comfort and sanctuary the quiet cathedral has tapped in her…ultimately she must find whatever it takes to meet the challenge of those forces seeking to destroy her from within herself. She suddenly feels claustrophobic, and hurries to the large wooden door to escape.

Fear clutches at her as she struggles to open the door, reminded of Viktor's break-in. Finally, after an several frantic tugs, she figures out the door and is out on the street, greedily sucking in the cool night air.

Carson is immersed in hot steamy water, his head resting on the towel he has rolled and placed on the back of the tub, and can feel the heat drawing the stress out of him. Sweat runs down his face, salty on his lips.

"I'm back." He can hear her puttering around.

"Can I come in?"

"Sure can."

She comes into the steamy bathroom, a glass of ice water in each hand, handing Carson one, and then sits on the toilet.

"Ok?"

"Yes. I've got a handle on it. But he does have a hold on me, Carson."

"Rome?"

"No. Viktor. And that says it all. I've confronted Rome head on; I can deal with him. I did deal with him. But with Viktor: I've only had one meeting with him, and it was, to say the least, very creepy. Since then, he has been invisible, while his mark seems to be on everything regarding this whole mess. At every step it seems that he has been there, but we can never know it for certain. He's a goddamned phantom!"

Raising his arms, Carson clasps his fingers behind his neck. "I know where he is."

"I think I do too."

"Where?"

"At Omar's."

Carson watches Morgan as she sits quietly, nodding to herself.

"So, Morgan. We visit him tomorrow. Time to get in his face…on our terms."

"Yes. Tomorrow."

With the idea in her head, Morgan feels better. The warm moist air feels good against her skin. She enjoys the interesting view she has of Carson.

"Want to get in?"

Morgan gets up and slips out of her dress, and carefully hangs it on the hook on the bathroom door. After taking off her underwear she folds them and puts them on the toilet lid. Carson makes room for her and she climbs into the tub, letting herself slip into the water until it floats against her chin. "Oh my! This is good."

The heat and moisture of the steamy bathroom are ruining the precision of Morgan's eye makeup, and she is looking more and more *Modiglianiesque* to Carson. He proffers his glass and she clinks hers against it.

"You make me happy."

"Time to take care of your thirst."

"Well, yes, it's that. But, drinking with a naked guy in a bathtub really helps."

"Ah. It's more than the glass half full."

"Definitely. It's the glass being filled full that I desire."

Carson wiggles his toes against her hip.

The water feels good against Morgan's skin. It also feels good to roll the glass across her forehead. Her eyes are closed as she starts talking: "This has become part of my life, hasn't it? I mean there's this pervasive threat of an attack that can happen at anytime. It must be how Angela feels…all the time."

"To me it's more that you go about life knowing that at any time you could come face to face with a violent situation."

"You're telling me I'm going to have to live with this?"

"For the time being."

Morgan nods, and then, closing her eyes and taking a breath, slips under the water, reappearing with her hair plastered to her head. Lifting her leg, she slips it over Carson's, and pushes her foot between his legs, wiggling her toes as she burrows.

The pressure of her toes feels good, He relaxes his legs, hoping she will push more.

"Feel anything?"

"Tiny Morgan?"

Morgan smiles, and, withdraws her foot from between Carson's legs, sliding it across him until her leg is draped over both of his.

She rests her head on the tub. "Yes. I need to confront Viktor. I need to go head to head with him like I did with Omar. It's the only way."

Sitting up, Carson runs his fingers through Morgan's damp hair, creating a path of dark spikes. "Look. I've had enough. Why don't you relax? I'll wait for you in bed, and we can play the married couple and read until we fall asleep."

"Yes. OK. I want to soak some more."

Leaning against a pile of carefully placed pillows, Carson puts his book down and watches Morgan as she rummages around in her suitcase, removing her cosmetic bag, and a small red stuff bag.

Before disappearing back into the bathroom she stops and gives him a tired smile. "Better."

Carson has read thirty pages before Morgan reappears, looking much the same except that her hair is dry and she is in her PJs-red bottoms and a white tank top. After getting a book from her tote bag, she arranges her pillows and gets into bed.

"I feel better."

Her eyes start to swim as soon as she opens her book. In the tub, alone, she had thought; a married couple-is that what he had said? Taking a washcloth from the side of the tub, she had put it over her face, soaking in the heat. *I guess some wives stew in the same tub brew as their husbands*. Tonight, being the wife sounded good…crawling into bed and feeling his hands on her, wrapping her legs around him. Tonight she wanted to lose herself with him. However, by the time she had dried her hair, brushed her teeth, and put on her pajamas, she hardly had enough energy to struggle into bed and close her eyes. Now, the page a blur through her half closed eyes, she can't remember what she said to Carson when she climbed in next to him.

"I think you're falling asleep. Why don't you turn off the light?" Morgan does not respond, so Carson takes her book, then reaches across her and turns off her light. "Night, night."

"M'mmm."

Carson rolls on his side away from Morgan after he puts his book on the nightstand and turns off the light. Sleep will be a shelter from their long day's effort to prevail over Omar and Viktor and make Morgan safe.

Morgan slides next to him; Carson can feel her body against his back, her breath on his neck. She rubs her body against him and pushes a leg between his and wraps an arm around him, slipping it under his arm-he finds her hand and holds it.

Sleepily slurring her words she mumbles, "Oh...my.... Why? You.... Ruined me? Be...nicer...after."

He waits. She does not speak again. Morgan trembles; then there is the unhurried breathing punctuated by an occasional breathy sigh.

Chapter Nine

One Man's Family

"There it is…just off to the right. It's that gravel road after the sign that says *O. Rome.*"

Carson slows down and eases their rental car (a Toyota *Yaris*) across the shoulder of the highway and onto the dusty gravel path. He can see a red tile roof over the rise to his left. Morgan is sitting next to him, map on her lap. She has been guiding him to Omar Rome's house; from Santa Fe on I25 heading to Las Vegas, and then about eight miles to the Lamy turnoff–US285. Several minutes ago, at the junction of State Highway 41, they headed toward Galisteo and then to the gravel road leading to Rome's place, and a confrontation with Viktor Perdu.

Morgan carefully folds the map and places it in the glove box. "Stop here for a minute."

Carson lets the Yaris coast, stopping it when the road dips and the house is out of view. He lowers the window halfway filling the car with dry heat borne on the whisper of a light breeze.

Morgan is struck by the incredible expansiveness of the sky, a huge blue canopy that seems to go on forever. Just as she thinks the Pacific Coast defines the spirit the Bay Area, she is sure this huge blue sky gives definition to all that stretches in all directions from Santa Fe.

"I'm more reassured after talking to Marc Sinclair and agreeing to have him fax our intentions to go legal, and putting both Rome and Perdu on notice that restraining orders are on the way."

"Yes."

Carson sighs. Putting the Yaris in gear, he eases it down the road, leaving a plume of dust telling the world of their arrival. Going another three quarters of a mile, the road rounds a bend, becoming paved, and after a short climb to the top of a knoll, they arrive at Omar Rome's timber and stucco territorial style house. It is a large square three-story main section with a two-story wing attached to each side. The wing on the side opposite the road has a large balcony running the entire width of its side. The entire house commands a view of the New Mexico plains that would be three hundred sixty degrees if it weren't for a small knoll rising about a hundred yards from the southwest corner of the mansion.

The road swings in front of a patio leading to the front door, ending in a small paved car park. Carson parks next to a black Range Rover, then, having second thoughts, with a series of quick maneuvers, repositions the car so that the front faces toward the road.

"Ready?"

Unlike her confrontation with Rome, Morgan has no story to tell Viktor.

Instead she must wrest his story from him and then render it meaningless-she must destroy his will to continue.

"Well, my heart is racing and I'm clammy all over. But other than that, I'm ready."

The patio is paved with sand colored flagstones with faint rose-colored veins running through them, a circular stone fountain in its center. Carson and Morgan linger to watch the water bubble from the top of a stone sphere, gliding down its sides into a large round pool. There are large pottery containers filled with flowers and succulents scattered around the patio.

Carson is surprised to see that the front door is ajar. "Look Morgan. The door is open."

"What does that mean?" Going to the door, Morgan peers through narrow opening. The interior is dark, quiet; indistinguishable features give it a foreboding atmosphere. "Strange." Morgan rings the doorbell and then steps back to wait beside Carson.

There are large narrow pained windows, each as tall as the large ornate wooden door, on each side of it, and Carson sees that one of the panes of the window on the left has a small hole in it, encircled by a dark red rosette.

"I think we better go in."

The sudden change in the tone of Carson's voice puts Morgan on guard.

Hesitating at the door he says, "Let's be very careful."

Morgan follows Carson into the dark, quiet interior. Carson's eyes are drawn to sunlight to his right and through a dark dining room he can see a kitchen. There is an acrid smell in the air, and he wonders if a teakettle or saucepan has been left over a flame or hot coil.

Strangely, the memory of her training in the Emergency Room flits across her memory before she realizes she smells the thick sweetness of blood. Almost simultaneously, her eyes now accustomed to the darkness, she sees a figure sitting on a sofa.

"Carson! Something's wrong!" Tentatively she enters what appears to be a very large living room.

"Morgan! Wait for me."

Morgan stops, waiting. She looks down in front of her, and in the dim, shadowy light sees a body sprawled at her feet.

Her scream pierces the silence. "Nooo!"

Carson fumbles along the wall next to the entrance of the room Morgan is in until he finds a light switch, flicking it on. The room flashes to brightness. Morgan retreats to Carson and clutches his arm. Unable to move, they can only stare, trying to understand the carnage they see before them.

"Oh Please! This can't be."

Morgan detaches herself from Carson. Viktor Perdu is sprawled on the floor in front of her, his torso surrounded by a congealed pool of blood that has seeped from him. Two gunshot wounds are burned into his back.

One of Viktor's legs is drawn up; per-haps he was running away when he was shot, or he raised it as close to his body as he could in a futile effort to dampen the pain from his wounds. An arm is thrown up in front of his face, long delicate fingers seem to be reaching, trying to touch or reach for something. The other arm stretches away from him, the hand half closed. Several feet away there is a pearl handled stiletto, a rusty red stain on the razor sharp edge of the blade.

Morgan squats beside Viktor, and sees two more wounds in his side, penetrating the soft part of his body just beneath his ribs. *God! He was shot four times.* Morgan is sure that each one would have killed him.

With a mix of trepidation and curiosity she looks at Viktor's face. Once handsome, it is now a rigid mask; his mouth is slack, and his lips, frozen in a grimace, have dried blood on them. Morgan remembers Viktor's eyes as a dark and mysterious brown, but, now, they have faded to dull sightless and staring yellow.

Her own gaze still fixed on Viktor's face, she thinks he did not die instantly-his body would try vainly to function, if only for a short time. However, the core of Viktor-his history, his thoughts and feelings, his hopes, his psyche ceased to exist as soon as the first bullet crashed through his body. Before he could blink, Viktor ceased to exist-and he never knew it.

Carson is looking at Viktor, too, and sees Morgan. His gorge rises at the similarity, forcing him to swallow rapidly. Except for the now colorless eyes, the shape of his face and eyes, his lips, the smoothness of his skin, and the shape of his nose are Morgan's. Only the small scars are missing. Blinking, he has to look away to force himself not to see the death mask as that of Morgan. *How can this be*?

Wordlessly, they move to the sofa where Omar Rome is sitting with his head slumped forward, giving the impression he is studying his wound, a small puncture

in his chest over his heart, a narrow
cascade of dried blood marring the blue
shirt, that had killed him. One hand rests
in his lap, the other, the right, grasps
a large caliber handgun.

He hears Morgan sigh. They continue to
stare.

Morgan thinks that, unlike Viktor, Omar
had time to contemplate his mortality before he died. As his life shrunk from
him, like a dying star collapsing into
itself, he knew he was dying. He knew he
had used the last of his life force for
one more act. Perhaps he used his remaining consciousness to contemplate what he
had done, perhaps to come to terms with
what had happened to him.

Looking at Carson, she says, "What happened here?"

Carson's reaction to Morgan's question
is, *Incredible! They've done the job for
us. Morgan is free*! But, he keeps his
thoughts to himself. Instead, he pushes
some sheets of paper that are scattered on
the floor between the two bodies with his

foot. "Marc's faxes. I think they argued. Both got backed up against the wall, and something snapped. For some reason Rome let Viktor get close, and Viktor stabbed him. It didn't kill Omar right off. He had enough left to shoot him. I think he had hidden a gun between the cushions of the sofa." *For self-defense, or had he planned to kill Viktor*?

"Viktor must have realized he hadn't killed Rome outright, and when he saw the gun he tried to escape."

Morgan wanders back to the fallen Viktor. She knows her inquisitiveness is masking a sense of horror. "Makes sense, I can't be sure, but the entry wounds in his back are angled up." She waves at the blood encrusted bullet hole in the window. "He was sitting when he shot Viktor. The wounds on Viktor's side are almost level, if not down a bit-those two came after he was on the floor."

Morgan turns back to Carson. "He really wanted to be sure he killed him."

"No doubt about that."

Carson has never seen violent death. However, here in the musty quietness of Rome's Villa, he knows he is in the firm grasp of death. It chills him to the bone, and as much as he wants to, he can't shake himself free of its dehumanizing hold on him. *Get out of here!* Then, taking a deep breath, he takes stock.

"Are you Ok? We have to be Ok."

Morgan nods that she is, but she's not so sure. Numb would be the best description. Numb in a surreal landscape. It is the absence of a grip on reality that is allowing her to cope.

Carson continues. "I don't think we have to call the police yet-there's certainly no hurry. Lets do a check of the house. We have to search, try to find out what these two were up to."

He senses hesitation from Morgan. "We have to do this…otherwise we'll never know."

A check of the empty house yields a partly packed suitcase in one of the bedrooms, and Omar Rome's passport with airline tickets to Oakland and to Mexico City from San Francisco, placed beside it. If it were not for the two bodies downstairs, it looks as if Omar was about to leave on a trip, a vacation, to Mexico. They find no evidence that Viktor lived in the house. There is a facsimile machine in another room, but no sign of a computer. However, when he checks his iPhone, he is asked if he wants to join the network *EnfantPerdu*, which requires a password.

Holding hands, they leave the house, stopping at the edge of the patio. Carson feels the heat of the sun on him, and wants it to purge the effects of death from him.

Still gripping his hand, Morgan is pulled to a stop when Carson stops. "Carson! What?"

"The ghost of Viktor Perdu the lost child."

Carson tilts his head toward what he thinks is a faint path leading away from the house and disappearing at a rise about thirty yards away. Searching, he sees an electrical line coming from the house and, supported by two wooden poles, disappearing over the rise. Pointing, he says, "I think that's a trail that leads over that rise. We better check."

"You're right. Viktor?"

"No signs of him living in the house, but there is a *wifi* signal."

At the rise they see an Airstream trailer nestled in a small depression. "Look Morgan…just as Omar's. The door is open." And, as they had done when they found the door to Omar's house ajar, they go in.

The compact space of the trailer's interior is neat and orderly. Morgan thinks that the trailer's orderliness reflects the compartmentalization of Viktor's mind. Once it was a young man's, a crazy young man's room where the placement of each object was in the service of maintaining the fragile balance of an otherwise chaotic and painful inner world. Now, however it is a mausoleum, and

Morgan imagines Viktor on the bed (under the covers to conceal his gapping wounds) arms folded across his chest, his long, brown hair framing his pale face.

"Morgan. You better take a look."

Propped against the wall are two bulletin boards, each covered with photos, newspaper clippings, letters, diagrams and charts. At first Morgan sees a mish-mash of random photos and memorabilia. Then there is recognition–not really recognition, but shock, the shock of seeing something that shouldn't be there, that existed in another universe, certainly not this present one.

"Carson. What am I looking at?"

Carson is looking at what appears to be a set-up for an investigation. In addition to the picture boards, there are documents stacked at the end of the bed and on a table at the end of the trailer. There is another table with a Dell laptop on it and a bulletin board leaning against the wall covered with notes, addresses, and more photos.

"You tell me."

Morgan leans closer to the board. "A photo of my father, and…" her voice trails off to silence. Next to him is an attractive woman with long blond hair. In front of the couple stands a young Viktor Perdu.

They move on, stopping in front of a faded newspaper clipping announcing the disappearance, and presumed death, of Gaston Alar while on a solo hike in the Sierras.

"I have a copy of this. It's telling of my father's disappearance in the Sierras."

Next to it is a clipping from a Swiss-German newspaper reporting on the progress of the search for Doktor Gaston Allard, who had disappeared while on a walk around Mont Blanc. Hesitantly Morgan translates for Carson.

"Your father died twice."

Numbly Morgan continues to scan the two bulletin boards, while in her mind a terrible canvas is taking shape, its images in the colors of Viktor's insane palette.

The second board has recent photos of her tacked to it…at Coles, Strada, Roma, a few of her in front of Café Simone deB… with Carson, with Blanca and Ari. Most of these are portraits–she and Carson, she and her two women friends. There are a few close-ups of her, and several of her in the act of crossing her legs or when she is wearing a short skirt that has ridden up.

The trail of photos ends with ones that she recognizes that are from her own albums, and she sees the archive box where she kept them at the end of the bulletin board.

"Viktor did it. He broke into my place and took a box of my photo albums. This is sick."

Then her gaze is pulled to an old photo, apart from the others. Beckoning to Carson, "And this? Who's this?"

Carson sees a man and a woman standing next to each other with a young boy that must be Viktor.

"Who are those people?"

"I don't know who the woman is. But the man next to her is my father."

"And the young guy is Viktor. Right?"

"No. I don't know who it is, but it's not Viktor."

Again, Carson is struck by the similarity. He is glad he is looking at this after Viktor. The young man in the photo is a boy Morgan. *We may not be out of the woods yet*.

"Ok, Morgan. Before I call 9-1-1, I'm going to photograph all this. While I'm doing that, copy all the files you can from Viktor's laptop."

"Ok. Don't forget to photograph all of my father's families—all three of them."

Closure

His name is Perry Anderson-his father is Gaston Allard. In an irony of fate, Morgan is his only known living relative, and becomes the executor of his estate.

Morgan had Perry's ashes flown to the Bay Area. Carson was with her at the Oakland Airport when his ashes arrived in the cargo hold of the United flight from Albuquerque. Ari and Blanca showed their disapproval by not participating.

At the Chapel of the Chimes where Morgan had purchased a niche, she said a few words.

"I am so relived this is finally over. I am still in a state of shock at the way it ended, at the same time depriving me of a brother, as crazy with hate as he was, while discovering another brother across the Atlantic."

Turning to Carson, she addressed him. "What I am sure of is that your friendship, your support, and your efforts on my part mean so much to me. I could not have survived without it. I promise I will make every effort to give you back what you have given to me.

"A large part of our lives is beyond our control. This part is relentless and uncaring when it comes to its effect on us. Occasionally it gives a gift: something with the potential to actually enrich our lives. I believe that when this happens we have to embrace it, and do what we can to make the best of it. I want my life back."

Chapter Ten

Out of the Mud Grows the Lotus[1]

To: M. le médecin Benoît Allard
From: Morgan Alar, M.D.
Subject: I'm Your Sister

I lost my father, Gaston Alar, when he went missing in the high Sierras. You lost Gaston Allard when he failed to return from a trek around Mont-Blanc. He was 48 years old: You were 25; I was 23.

My father left me half (torn in two, lengthwise) of a crayon and graphite sketch on light brown paper. My half-the right side-is part of a slender, shadowy figure in

---

1.   Buddhist value.

motion…he is walking off my page.
It could be a Giacometti; it could
be a Picasso. It bears no signature
so it could be a good forgery. It is
carefully torn—about 40 cm at the
top, 24 cm at the bottom. The figure
is roughly 61 cm tall. On the back,
there are parts of strings of numbers and three letters: *Mar*….

I want to join the halves…cre-
ate a new family portrait. Please
e-mail me; I am eager to meet you at
long last.

Morgan

P.S. We have a brother.

Morgan looks at her watch; in fifteen
minutes she will have a *FaceTime* conversation with Carson. She is alone at her
place at Stinson Beach. She had no desire to return to her studio, settling

in instead at Stinson, commuting to Café Simone deB.

She remembers that it took fifteen minutes of driving in silence after leaving Omar's villa for the numbness to dissipate. Just as Carson turned onto the freeway, Morgan realized that that she was no longer in danger for her life. Viktor and Omar had taken it in their own hands to close out the final chapter. They had spent a frantic time in Viktor's trailer, copying, downloading, and e-mailing to themselves, everything they could that seemed to relate to Viktor's mysterious, and crazy, vendetta against her, as well as Gaston Allard's family portraits before calling the police.

She remembers the wave of relief that washed over her. She felt buoyant; there was the sensation of floating, gently restrained by her seatbelt. Then she remembered Viktor sprawled at her feet. She had turned to Carson.

"Viktor is my brother."

"I think that, too."

"Stop the car, Carson."

As quickly as he could Carson slowed the car, bringing it to a stop on the shoulder of the freeway. Getting out, she walked until she was past the road debris into a pristine landscape. The breeze was warm and strong enough make the shrubs around her quiver. A city girl, she did not know their names, but they seemed to belong. Carson caught up with her, and they stood, silent, gazing in to the vast stretch of desert.

Turning to him she says, "I'm different."

"How?"

"It's hard to describe. When I said to you that Viktor was my brother, I was telling myself, also. I felt a shudder, like something inside me had shifted. I was the same, but at the same time my experience of all that has happened seemed different-same old pieces, I guess, just grouped together differently.

Except now I own the experiences of the events involving Omar Rome, and, ah, my brother. I feel very strongly that I can carry these forward in a way that will make sense of what happened with the result that I will have a clearer view of myself."

"Your experience of what happened is now stronger than the impact of each event on you, and this shift gives you a clear sense of yourself."

"Yes, in a way that resonates. The past is still there, but it doesn't tug at me as it did. Or perhaps better, the past has different meaning because I'm different."

They stood for a while in silence until the harshness of the desert began to punish them, forcing then to return to the car.

Morgan checks her watch. *Five minutes*. She hurries to the bathroom to check…she had showered and then fixed her hair a bit and put on some eye make-up, and got into her new French pajamas. Then she hurries to the bedroom, hopping on the bed in front of her MacBook Pro.

Carson checks his watch. *Five minutes.* Back in the Bay Area, Morgan had immediately moved to her place at Stinson. Her new schedule is to commute to Simone deB Tuesday through Thursday, spending the long weekend there.

So far dinners, dates, and sleepovers have not found their way into the schedule. Instead it's coffee at Roma before work, hanging out between patients, lunch (not at Zachary's), and *FaceTime* calls a couple of times during the weekend.

Carson reflects on Morgan's resilience. Back from New Mexico she had hit the ground running, easily making important decisions, while throwing herself back into daily life in the Bay Area.

He thinks that at sometime during the recent series of events Morgan began a deconstruction process. Perhaps it was started by the deaths of Viktor and Omar and ended in a reconstruction of a same yet very different Morgan (Could it have been, as she believes, the realization that Viktor is her brother?). Anyway, it seems that she has incorporated the experience of the events in such a way that she now has power over them, and dealing with them she can use her experience of them to carry her forward rather than being held back by them. *Interesting*.

He remembers an incident of long ago; it was in another physical time, but the experience is still with him, and when he remembers, it is as fresh as the day it happened.

It was a lake in the Sierras-a fisherman's lake high in the back-country. Several families are on a camping trip before the start of spring practice (Carson's father followed the National League schedule). He and his best friend Larry were the first ones in the lake, much colder than he had expected, and they decided to slow down and wait for the other kids. Suddenly Larry began thrashing about–Carson thought he was playing around but suddenly he quieted down, and then, his eyes riveted on Carson, disappeared beneath the surface.

Carson remembers a frantic swim to the spot where Larry went down, and diving, and diving, and diving again into the cold water, clear on the surface and murky green underneath, holding his breath until it was almost too late, above long grasses waving slowly, and bleached logs resting in the sand on the bottom that he took for Larry. He remembers being pulled from the lake by his father and another man, and struggling to break from their grasp and dive under again. The rescue team found Larry's body the next day.

The images occur less and less, but they still occur. They occur during times of stress, of vulnerability, of insecurity, or by surprise as if it is time to be reminded that it did happen, and make him struggle with his feelings of loss and failure. They are not as powerful now, they do not control or define him anymore-rather they are background noise that seeps into his existential being from time to time.

Will it be the same for Morgan regarding Viktor Perdu and Omar Rome? Will the events grab at her, making her doubt herself? Then will the events dim and become part of the background of her experiences, part of her memories? He wonders. Perhaps not. Maybe he has confused memory with experience. Perhaps Morgan has taken a step that he has not. Perhaps the memories return the way they do because they are memories still searching for an emotional connection. Does the event of the lake still need a joining with his experience of it to make it whole so he can come to a meaningful understanding and acceptance of it? Carson thinks there is another step yet to come for him—some kind of shift that will make an as yet unknown change possible.

He gets on his bed, opens *FaceTime*, and, after highlighting and clicking on Morgan's e-mail address waits for the computers to go through their connection process. A virtual Morgan appears, sitting on her bed in her new French pajamas. The screen image has a yellow-orange tinge from the incandescence of her bedroom lights.

"Whoa! Here you are on the end of my bed."

"Hey! Strange. You're on the end of my bed, too. How's it going?"

"Good. The overcast never went away, so I hung around here…writing case notes…reading. You?"

"Sunny here. Went to the Farmers' Market in the City, played some basketball. By the way, Jon Cade e-mailed me…from Seattle. He and Leda have split. He's driving down here."

"Really? Well, can't say I'm surprised. She leave him?"

"Right. I'll know more when he gets here, but she's in Switzerland with that guy Martin. How are you doing?"

"Not bad at all."

"Are you going ahead with your plan to contact Benoît?"

"Yes. I'm working on it now. I think looking to the future, looking forward to meeting my brother strengthens me with my issues around losing Viktor…as crazy as that sounds."

"It doesn't sound crazy. It's a family thing. You and Benoît…there's strength in that."

"Yes. Comfort, too."

"Did you get the attachment I sent you?"

"Yes."

Morgan reaches for a sheet of paper that is resting on a pillow behind her. It's a sketch of a family tree. Starting from the bottom of the page are the names, Benoît, Morgan, and Perry (Viktor), each in their own boxes. Perry's name has a discreet gray line through it. Each name is connected to another box: Marie (Last name?) for Benoît, Maria Alvarado for Morgan, and Adele Anderson for Perry. The three women are connected to the lone box at the top of the diagram: Gaston Allard. Gray lines pass through the boxes of the three women and Gaston Allard, and there is a question mark sitting outside Allard's box. Morgan tosses the paper to the side.

"One man's families. You think he's alive, don't you?"

"Well, he'd be sixty-three. What we do know is what's detailed on the family tree. Then there are the airplane tickets of Omar and Viktor. They were planning to be in the Bay Area for a short time, and then each was going in a different direction. The start date is in about a week. I did find some e-mail notices from the Bank of the West. On four occasions twenty-five thousand dollars was deposited and then almost immediately withdrawn. The last two withdrawals were a day before we went to Santa Fe."

"I'm still amazed how he found us."

"A person like Viktor, fueled by his obsessions, had the energy to spend hours and hours gathering information, and then putting all the puzzle pieces together-and scheming."

"Carson-how are you?"

"Actually, pretty good. Pretty solid-getting back to work and back in the community, and looking forward to hanging out with Cade has grounded me. I'm still trying to wrap my mind around the events, but it's not the only thing I do.

"Sometimes I feel as if something is wrong, and that makes me feel like I've fucked-up in some way, but struggling with it isn't so bad because I know I'll get through it. I'm beginning to see what we have gone through as a forging process, and that I, we, are stronger, you know, more tempered, and…what can I say: Out of the mud grows the lotus."

"When we were in the midst of our events, we did our best. Now we're drawing strength from our experience."

"Yes, that makes sense. I'll probably never stop dealing with what we went through, but, at the same time, I'll be drawing strength from it for a long time, too."

The data stream is slow and Carson watches Morgan languidly take hold of the bottom of her pajama top, one image blurring into the next until it is done.

She lifts the bottom of her PJs revealing a narrow swatch of skin, before tugging it down, stretching it as far as she can. He has seen the motion before, usually when she is feeling threatened, most often by Viktor. She sighs.

"What?

"Viktor is still in my head.

"What do you mean?"

"Now and then…moments like this…I feel like someone is snapping photos of me, or recording what I'm saying. It's really an icky feeling."

Carson does not know what to say, but Morgan fills the silence.

"He was so perverse…he stole my privacy. Right now I can imagine people in front of other computers, watching me, listening to me."

"I understand. He sucked you into his crazy world where privacy did not exist."

"Unguarded moments. Has my life become a series of unguarded moments?"

"He's gone Morgan."

Morgan sighs again, and staring into the camera, shrugs her shoulders.

"Tell me I'm being irrational."

"Well, I guess you are. But, who wouldn't be, given what you've been through. Really though, it's just you and me. Just you when you want, and you share only what you want to."

"I've got to get that sucker out of my head."

"You will."

"I know. It just won't be soon enough…. Coffee Tuesday morning?"

"See you at Roma."

"Night, night, Carson. Sleep tight."

"You too, Morgan."

Carson watches Morgan reach for her computer, watching her image fade before he closes off the connection.

Chapter Eleven

Two Conversations

To: Carson
From: Morgan
Subject: GB

Before I left on Thursday I went to a BAKS meeting–the Gloria Belknap interview was the topic. I won't bore you with the details, but it was a disaster…for her. No one wanted her in the group but everyone seemed content to analyze her rather than saying so. When I suggested a vote, everyone got very concerned about what they referred to as possible Legal Action. The discussion finally died with one of the members agreeing to talk with an attorney, leaving me at the point of screaming. What a bunch of chumps! God! It seemed I was the only one with balls. Anyway, get ready for the e-mails.

Morgan

At Peaberrys? When?

"I asked for that." Carson puts his iPhone on the table by their coffees.

"Gloria?"

"Yeah. Summoned. She's doing what I did, asking for a meeting at Peaberrys."

"Are you going?"

"I guess so. It's part of the détente; she hasn't fired off an e-mail since our last meeting."

"Do you have to go now? We just got here." *And haven't seen each other in four days*…she feels like the jealous girlfriend. They are on one of the wooden benches in the small terrace of Roma, on the College Avenue side of the café. The sun is out, and soon it will be warming them. Carson had walked from his digs—Morgan had driven in from her place at Stinson Beach.

"An hour. I'll tell her an hour." Picking up his mobile, he sends Gloria the text message, and then slips the mobile into the front pocket of his jeans. He notices that Morgan is wearing jeans, too; she has been wearing them to Simone deB since their return from Santa Fe.

They both stare at their *au laits*, which are, as they are at Strada, small *lattes*, their absence from each other leaving them estranged, and they need to reconnect—they need to seek a new starting point that is comfortable. Carson, pulling on his ear, breaks the silence.

"Did you send the e-mail?"

"I did. I used the folder you gave me with the info we found in Viktor's trailer. I guess I should call him Perry—it's hard though after all he put us through in the name of Viktor.

"Anyway, Benoît is a medical doctor, an internist and he's Swiss which makes sense because our father is Swiss. He's living in Paris with his boyfriend, Didier DuLac. Didi has a place in the eighth, near Étoile."

Carson raises his eyebrows. "Nice digs I would guess." He is aware that Morgan has used the term, our father, and had referred to Gaston Allard in the present tense…as if he is still among the living.

Morgan continues, "I also found out that Benoît has published several articles in what seem to be juried journals. He's raising the bar for me. Anyway, their focus is AIDS.

"I wrote the e-mail in English."

"Staking out your territory?"

"Some of that. I didn't want to seem a smart-ass American girl. Hey look at me. I went to college and learned French."

"Family matters. New and blended—you have to find a starting point that you can build on."

Morgan nods. "Yes." *Just like us.* "Any word from Cade?"

"He has some business in Seattle, then he's going to come down here…stay in the city for a couple of days before he comes over here. He's looking at a condo near the tunnel…Parkwood, or something like that. I told him he could crash at my place."

Carson leans back, resting his back on the wall of the café, wondering if he sees tiny worry lines near Morgan's eyes. "How are you doing? You know…how are you processing the recent events?"

Even though she has anticipated Carson's question-she knew it would be a matter of time before he asked-it still sends a shiver of anxiety through her, however the anxiety sharpens her attention.

"I'm changing my ways…habits, I guess. I'm keeping my iPhone on and in my purse-actually today I've taken a lesson from you, it's in my jean's pocket-keeping my spray handy, too, and being vigilant, sometimes I'm hyper-vigilant."

"Hyper-vigilant. I know what you mean. I notice so much more…always looking, wondering, searching for patterns."

"That's right. And, looking for what seems out of place. I've thought about this quite a bit, especially at my Stinson place.

"At first I thought I was too much in my head, you know, staying away from my feelings. But, I realized I…we…had been in the trenches, and totally just trying to take care of ourselves, to survive, and that now it was time to make sense of the experience."

"What did you come up with?"

"At first I told myself that it was over, that we were beyond all the bad stuff and could now get on with our lives. But, I soon realized that was not so.

"I've lived a privileged life and now that's over. For me life was always out there, beckoning to me, and there was a plan: become a doctor, practice medicine, achieve status in the community, have a relationship with a man. In short, I could have what I want. What has happened is that lived life has trumped the planned life, the expected life. I can't put life behind me. There will always be obstacles, surprises, roadblocks, and especially detours that will throw me off the grid. It's the life my patients struggle with, why shouldn't I?"

"We're changed…and we'll change again and again. It's all trenches…the same as for everyone else."

"Can't go back. Don't want to." Morgan runs her fingers through her hair and red highlights flash in the morning sun that is filling the terrace. She thinks of telling him of her plans, but decides that later would be better. Instead, "Talking is good…."

The conversation falters, and there is a zone of silence between them. Morgan leans forward, taking hold of Carson's proffered hands. "Is it time?"

Looking at his watch: "Ok. Got to get going." Getting up, Carson gathers his jacket and backpack.

"I'm going to sit here for a while."

"Ok. See you later." He leaves the terrace, turning onto College, and stops opposite Morgan peering at her over the barrier of greenery that separates them.

"Stay at my place tonight."

"Yes. But, I'll just show up…Ok?"

"Shall I fix something for us?"

"That would be nice."

"With candlelight?"

"That would be very nice."

Gloria

Carson finds an outside table at Peaberrys, and after checking out the comings and goings of the market crowd for a while, goes to the counter and orders a mocha and a cappuccino. Returning to the table, he places the mocha across from him. He hears bracelets jingling against each other before he sees her, and then, after moving the chair closer, she is sitting next to him.

"Carson! You are so sweet. It's so nice to have one's every need anticipated."

Today Gloria's color pallet is in the blue spectrum—light to dark, matte to glossy. Carson notices that unlike Morgan, there are small worry wrinkles forming near her eyes, and even though her hair and make-up are perfect, she looks a bit off kilter. *Coming unglued*?

"Hey, Gloria. What's up?"

"I love texting. Don't you? I say to myself, It has been a week. Time to check in with Carson. A few taps, and, *Voila!* Here we are an hour later." Her laugh is a melodious trill, but seems forced.

"It does work, I'll say that. By the way, thanks."

"My pleasure." Gloria scoops some whipped cream from her mocha and sucks it from her spoon, leaving some in the corner of her mouth. She is serious now, no more gaiety, no more double entendres; instead her look is one of anguish.

"Any news?"

"News?"

"You know. BAKS. Do you know anything?"

"I really don't have any details."

Gloria sighs. "Very sexist. There was so much testosterone in the room. I think they were against me from the start. Can you do anything for me…put in a good word?"

"Look. I'm sorry the interview may have been loaded against you. But, I really have nothing to do with that group." Gloria starts to protest, but he continues, "I know. I know Morgan is, but she does not tell me anything about BAKS's goings on."

Gloria sighs. "I knew you'd say that. It's just that…that…."

She sighs again. "I'm going through some hard times."

"I'm sorry."

"I tell my patients that their life is like a puzzle and they need to piece it together, and then work to hold it together. Obviously there are gaps, pieces that are missing, but part of the job is the search to find the ones that fit and then grab on to them and hold on to them."

"I get it."

"I tell my supervisees the same thing, except I hold them to higher standards. That is, I have my standards and they must meet them."

Carson nods that he is listening.

"I refused credit to some of my supervisees who did not meet my standards. I wrote them letters telling them so. They complained to the department chair. Now people, a faculty committee, are nosing around, asking questions. They're reviewing my evaluations, and asking my supervisees to write new ones. They're even talking to the agencies where the supervisees have placements." Gloria stops and is silent, and in the silence Carson thinks that she has got herself into a mess. She probably thinks people are coming after her, and, this time, she is most likely right.

"I work hard for what I get…so very hard, and when I'm successful, someone always tries to steal it from me."

The trouble with her puzzle is that it has no boundaries, and if pieces don't fit, it's their fault.

"People are threatened by who I am, what I am capable of, and what I accomplish. But you know? You know I can fight back. I will fight back. No one is going to steal from me. Woe to anyone who tries!

"And, I'm a good therapist. I'm a really good supervisor. Really good: even if sometimes I have to tell them things, do things that they may not like. Do you understand?"

"I do understand. You have a lot of irons in the fire, and they are all demanding you attention. Not an easy…."

"I thought you would understand. I'm going through a hard time…I need you to be supportive."

"I do understand."

"I trust you. You're very important to me."

Gloria abruptly changes directions. "You know, that free-be dinner invitation is still being offered."

"That's very gracious, but I have to say no. No thank you."

Carson sees that Gloria's face is flushed, down to the opening of her blue silk shirt, and there is a thin line of sweat on her upper lip. She leans close, and whispers, "I want you to be my friend."

Carson knows what she's asking.

"I won't tell."

"I can't do that, Gloria."

Gloria frowns and then pouts. "You're not making this easy." She sighs and then smiles, batting her eyes at him: "What does a girl have to do?"

"It not you. Really. Morgan and I are very attracted to each other, and we're trying to make it work."

"I hope you're not being dense on purpose. Can't you see a win-win opportunity when it's smack in front of you?"

"I take seriously what you are saying... I understand. It just won't work for me."

Gloria's smile, frozen on her face since her arrival dissolves. Her voice has an edge, but rather than angry her face is terribly strained with confusion. "You call me for a coffee date, and then you come when I invite you. Now when I open myself to you, you reject our relationship."

"I have rejected what you propose. It's not how I want things to go."

Gloria fidgets with her purse, and Carson thinks she is going to leave. When she looks up at him, he sees a wildness to her, especially in her eyes and the set of her mouth-in an instant she seems a different person...one Gloria has gone, another has taken her place.

"That's just blatant psycho-babble bullshit, Carson. I get it. Don't you? Don't you get it? You're just a cover for her sick desires-her prurient attachment to Ari Hawkins and Blanca Lane. I think the French have a word for it, *ménage* à *trois*. You're window dressing...for a sick threesome."

"Can we leave Morgan out of this? She's not here to defend herself."

"Why do you persist in defending her?" Gloria puts her hands under her breasts, lifting them toward him. "I have much more to offer, I'm much more a woman…more passionate, more sensitive, more intelligent than that thief, that anorexic bitch."

Carson does not respond. They have leaned closer to each other, and have not raised their voices. *I haven't handled this well at all…what's coming next*? There is the trill of laughter and the frozen smile returns.

"Ok. I get it. Poor baby. I intimidate you, is that it? Sooo sorry. You need some space? Ok…I'll give you some space. I know you'll be back."

With a heavy sigh and a shake of her head, Gloria gathers her things, and starts to leave, but stops. "It's not you, you know, I like bad boys." She leans close to him, and he is afraid she is going to try to kiss him. Instead, she whispers in his ear, "Change your mind… give in to it…or you'll be sorry. So very sorry."

Chapter Twelve

Morgan Alar

Gloria Sends a Message:

Subject: Have You Missed Me?

No news on the BAKS selections yet. But, I can tell you that my interview was thick with testosterone-two old white guys with gray beards in the room with me. I had to work very hard; I felt invisible.

Speaking of gray beards, I saw Bernie's daughter, Blanca, walk-ing arm in arm with Morgan Alar the other day. They were going into Whole Foods. I wonder where Carson Arrowsmith fits into this?

Anyway, I'm beginning to get it. That is, why Morgan named her medical clinic Simone de Beauvoir.

Morgan and Carson

"Carson? You awake?"

"Yes."

Tangled in each other's arms, in the silent hours of the night they retreat to their memories. Then Morgan untangles herself from Carson.

"Got to pee." Morgan slides from the bed, and in the defuse glow of the early dawn light that is filling the studio, crosses the room and disappears into the bathroom.

First we survive the attempted revenge of Viktor and Omar Rome. Now, I'm sure, Gloria is gearing up for a serious attack on us. Another test.

He watches as she comes back to bed, padding across the rugs and parquet. *Definitely Modiglianiesque.*

Morgan scoops up Carson's gray T-shirt and black shorts, stopping to put them on before hopping back into bed, landing on her knees, leaning close to Carson.

She puts a hand on his chest. "Carson? How are you doing?"

Carson knows what she means. He sighs. "Well, I'm still hyper-vigilant, always checking my surroundings, checking out people, looking for assassins, I guess. I spend a lot of time rummaging through the stuff we got from Viktor's trailer, trying to make sense of it all. I'm off balance."

"And...?"

"When I go through times like these, I start thinking and dreaming about events where I failed or came up short, events that made feel less than...."

"Maybe you should give an example."

"I go over the collision at second again and again. The guy really took me out. I had hit a homerun in our half of the inning, and I think he was out to get me. I probably could have avoided it...I don't know why I didn't.

"Anyway, I expected an explosion from my dad, but there wasn't one. In fact, there was nothing. Instead, while I was recovering he started working with my younger brother, Sean, who eventually replaced me at second. In times like these a phrase keeps running through my mind–a repeating loop. Now playing second base, and replacing Carson Arrowsmith…Sean Arrowsmith."

"Your brother replaced you."

"Because I was stupid and didn't get out of the way. I have to say that when I was a senior and gave up trying to please my father, the event lost its clout and the tape stopped playing. It has come back, though."

Morgan is silent. She realizes she was always careful not to let her father down; it was not an option. She is aware that what Carson went through must have been devastating. She reaches under the covers and, finding his hand, takes hold of it, squeezing hard.

"The thing with my father seems to run with another more recent event. It probably relates to us. When I was in grad school, I had a girlfriend, Sibley. She had a best friend, Roxie, and the three of us would hang out together. There was a coolness between Roxie and me, and I wasn't sure whether it was because of Sibley, or that she didn't like me. The issue came up with Sibley, and she told me that it wasn't dislike or because of her. Rather, Roxie found me uninteresting. She thinks you're a cardboard cutout, Sibley told me.

"A couple of years after we all finished our degrees, I happened to meet Roxie at a convention in San Diego. Sibley had e-mailed both of us, and we were on the lookout for each other. I asked her to dinner, and afterwards we took a walk on the beach. While we were walking she told me I had changed…that I was different.

"I said, Not a cardboard cutout? And she said, No, not a cardboard cutout. Anyway, she asked for a hug, and afterwards we walked back to the hotel and to our rooms."

"Was there more?"

"No. It seemed done to me, and there's been nothing since. But, I think the cardboard cutout thing still grabs at me. It's strange, but those few words have staying power."

"Carson. I'm so sorry. I've needed you and leaned on you so much through all this, and all the while this thing has been messing with you, dredging up old hurts and making you question yourself."

A chill runs through her, making her shudder even though she is not cold. Rather, the chill is in her psyche, a shudder due to the series of events they have just endured that has reached to the very core of their being, threatening their existence.

"Listen to me. As your lover I have privileges, especially the one that allows me to tell you nice things about yourself.

"You are not…definitely not…a cardboard cutout. Quite the opposite. You have quite a presence, and come across very well defined–attentive…engaged. When you invited me to your hotel room that night in Paris, I agreed…without hesitation."

Carson takes her hand, kissing it. "That means a lot to me. Whatever the past, whatever others think of me, your thoughts and feelings mean the most."

She flops down next to him. "Believe me?"

"Yes I do."

"And it continues despite all that has happened since. We must really like hanging out together."

"You bet. We're real."

Morgan reaches across Carson, looking at his watch. "What time is it? It's four-thirty. I'm wide awake."

"I'll make some coffee." Carson gets out of bed. Morgan is wearing his shorts and shirt, so he goes to the sofa and pulls on his jeans and the T-shirt he was wearing when they had dinner. Next he folds the screen that usually separates the bed from the rest of the studio and turns on some lights, chasing the night away, hurrying the start of day.

Morgan watches him remembering how lean and hard his body feels when she is wrapped around him. Now turned in-house *barista*, he is busy making their morning coffee.

"I got a text from Gloria."

Carson stops his coffee preparations. "Really? What'd she say?"

"That you were playing fast and loose with her and me, and that we needed to talk."

"She's gearing up for an assault."

"Do you know what this is about?"

"I think so. At Peaberry's she suggested that we should start a discreet relationship. When I said I couldn't do that, she began to decompensate. She said that I would be sorry." Carson goes back to his preparation.

"Ok. I guess I should talk to her."

Carson nods his agreement as he finishes up.

She would like to have her coffee with Carson in bed. But the dishes and glasses and the rest of the setting from dinner are still on the table, as well as some saucepans on the stove, and an ice bucket and empty bottle on the counter next to the sink. Kicking off the covers, she starts to get up.

"Hey! Stay there…it's the best place for our morning coffee."

"What about the kitchen?"

"It waited for us last night, it can wait for us now." After putting her coffee on her nightstand, he slips in next to her.

Morgan and Benoît

Carson. Can we meet…soon? I've just talked to Benoît.

Coles? In an hour?

See you there.

Morgan dabs at the tears that continue to well up. The whole event had caught her by surprise. She had switched off the ringer of her iPhone when she was at Carson's place and had not turned it back on so she had no idea what to expect when she got to Simone deB and awakened her Mac.

They had been up so early that even after coffee there was time for Carson to walk to La Farine for croissants to go with the second coffee that they had while reading the Chronicle that he also brought back. Even so, she had arrived before Pru and been alone in the office when she saw the e-mail–what caught her eye was the service provider: *orange.fr*. Written in French, it was from Didier DuLac.

The e-mail started by saying that she really had got their attention, filling them with both anticipation and dread. The e-mail went on to say that the information she had given them gave her a good deal of credibility. However, could she offer anything more concrete, more graphic? Then in English: I'm sorry, but we must up the ante. Could she send a photo of her half of the print?

Didier had sent his message at three in the afternoon their time. Now two hours later, it was late afternoon in Paris. Morgan reasoned that if she replied immediately, Didier could be at his computer, and, perhaps would reply soon after reading her message. Changing her keyboard to a French one, she wrote a short note saying how happy she was to receive his e-mail.

She and Carson had prepared a file for just such a situation, including not only family photos but also a photo of her half of the print, as well as copies of the newspaper articles reporting their father's death and Viktor's death, and she sent it as an attachment.

At three o'clock-midnight in Paris-there was a brief reply. It said *Skype*? There was a Paris phone number. She checked the time, and then sent a brief reply: *Have a patient…one hour.*

Her camera image, in its small window looked fairly normal–she had turned off the lights and opened the shades–even though it was in its own time-space continuum, mirroring her a few clicks after she moved. There was the metallic sound of ringing, and a larger window opened on her screen revealing the image of a man in his late thirties or early forties. His black tie was loosened its color in stark contrast to his white shirt, his hair was cut short and was reddish brown–mostly red–and she watched him as he removed his rimless glasses and stared into the camera. He had sensitive eyes and a man of the world look that she found attractive. He spoke the first words–rapid French with a Southern accent.

"Oh! Oh my God! I have twins. I'm Didi."

"*Morgan. I am so glad you decided to talk in person. This is the first good event in what seems an endless stream of bad ones.*"

"I can agree. You are the only positive in what seems a sea of negatives. However, we are ready to take the risk. Please understand that we are eager but cautious at the same time."

Didi's hesitant image slides from its window, and after a few thumping heartbeats thudding against Morgan's ribcage, a new image fills the space–Morgan understands what *Didi* meant when he exclaimed that he had twins. Her brother is a mirror image…almost. His dark hair, casually parted in the middle frames a narrow, pale face, and falls against the collar of his black T-shirt. His eyes are shaped like hers and are dark, his nose is like hers, a bit larger, and he has the same thin lips as she does. He looks tired, stressed, even. She wonders if he is seeing the same.

"Benoît?"

Nodding, he replies in English.

"Indeed, This is so strange. I am seeing my long lost sister for the

first time even though I did not know
I had one until several days ago.
It's strange that one is often eager to establish a safe harbor away
from all that would be upsetting
and unsettling. Then something like
this comes along, and one wonders if
what can seem upsetting can also be
something that like the sun after a
storm that allows you to bask in it
and it warms you."

Morgan thinks that Benoît has rehearsed
his first statement. His accent has a soft
British lilt to it, and Morgan assumes
his native language is Swiss-German,
and that he learned his English from a
British tutor, or even in England. She is
sure he speaks French, and wonders about
his choice of speaking English to her.
She wishes she had thought about what to
say to Benoît when they met for the first
time.

"The events leading to this have
happened so quickly that my thoughts
and feelings have yet to catch up.

But one thing I know I want is that regardless of what our father did, we give ourselves a chance."

"I want to agree with you. I don't mind telling you, though, that my life is complicated enough, and finding out I have a younger sister only increases the complexity."

"I will try to be a good baby sister."

"I want to believe you, but I've heard baby sisters will say anything."

This repartee causes Benoît to smile for the first time, and it seems to create a thaw in the mood of the conversation.

"I agree that I have the advantage. I have found you and am tying to get into your life knowing more about you than you know about me. But when I saw those photos in Viktor's trailer, there was no doubt in my mind that I must find you. I knew I must find you even if nothing comes of it except that we know of each other."

"I have resisted this from the instant I read your e-mail. But I have talked with Didi, and now that you are in front of me and I can see you and hear your voice, and listen to you, I know you are right."

"I have no expectations."

"What if this is to be our only conversation?"

"I can accept that. I would be disappointed, of course, but the circle would be complete. I would not only have Viktor, I would have you, too."

"Viktor. It is hard for me to have any feelings…."

"I can accept that. But I saw him dead. I saw the blood that poured from him congealed around him on a cold stone floor–Alar blood…our blood."

Morgan remembers worrying that she is being too emotional, and running the risk of chasing Benoît away. Then, staring at the screen, she watches him frown and purse his lips and memories of her father return, remembrances of times when he did the same and she worried that she had gone too far and was going to chase him away. Then, there is another thought. *Do I do that, too?* Glancing at her image, she sees furrowed eyebrows, pursed lips. *Shit! This is not going to be easy.* Benoît pulls her back to Paris.

"Later. Viktor can come later. But now, our father, let's talk about Gaston Allard. What was it like between you two?"

"Well, we waited. My mother and I waited for our father to return from his business trips, now, I assume, returning from spending time with his other family…that is, with you. He would bring gifts; we would take a trip to Taos, sometimes to Albuquerque.

"Then we would settle into a pattern at home. He would putter around the house, and would spend our evenings at home, reading, doing puzzles, playing dominos. He and I would also spend time together, hiking, going to the Plaza in Santa Fe. Those were special times for me. There would be a lot of talk, and he would gently instruct me on various things."

"Did he tell you about his trips?"

"No. And, I never thought to ask. I do not remember my mother asking. While he was home, we were a happy little family, and I was a happy daughter, reading books and talking about them, doing a lot of French and German, little lectures on the importance of this or that, and out-ings with my mother or just alone with him. Then, at dinner one eve-ning he would announce that he would have to be gone for a while."

"Did you go away to school? What then."

"I spent my high school years in Switzerland. I think I went home the summer after the first year, but after that, I didn't really go home again, rather vacations were for travel, mostly France. You?"

"Sounds like my story. Only it was French and English, and there was football and tennis. There was never a doubt that I would study medicine and become a doctor. Do you think about him?"

"Maybe after he went missing; now and then as the years passed. After Omar Rome, came into my life I thought about him a lot. At first he just rattled around in my head, making me anxious, then, when I found about Viktor, and tried to make sense of things, I got angry, I'm still mad at him, but mostly I'm questioning myself. I have been working hard to invent who I am, and I believe there's some of me, stuck in my unconscious, that was invented by him. It's an unsettling feeling."

"Well, if that's true for you, it must be true for me, too."

So different. So different, yet so much alike, were Morgan's thoughts as she listened to Benoît. He also looked anxious… wound tight, like a spring at maximum. *Am I that way too*? *Would Carson say I was wound tight*? At this point she decided to take a risk.

"You look stressed, Benoît."

"I do? Well perhaps you're right. Of course, if I am you must accept some of the blame. But of course there is more. I am Swiss. Didi is French. Where will we settle? I'm here on a grant to do AIDS research, but only for a year and a half more. And, I'm at a small clinic in Belleville. In America you have Americans of all kinds, and they have their advocate groups. In France it seems there are French and, well, non-French, and it is not easy to be French and something else. None of this was a topic of my father's lectures."

"But he did talk about marriage, money?"

"Most certainly. He was very adamant that while money should not be valued for itself, it was very necessary for independence, which would allow me the freedom of creating my own life. He was also very adamant that I should marry, and that my wife would be a woman who would support my goals, and create a comfortable home for us and our children."

Then he smiled one of his few smiles and said, Actually France's gift to me is a supportive husband. This had got a hoot from Didi, who took advantage of being mentioned to scoot in front of the camera with Benoît and into the conversation. The conversation from this point on became a slipping in and out of French and English.

The thought of Didi makes Morgan smile. Very effervescent, he laughed a lot and asked a lot of questions. She could see that his energy powered up Benoît, allowing him to relax and be more expressive. *Cute couple*, she thinks.

Taking over the conversation Didi wanted to know if she had a boyfriend or girlfriend.

"*I have a boyfriend.*"

"*Do you live together?*"

"*He says we're a rockin and a reelin.*"

"*Comment?*"

"*No. We aren't living together. I guess you could say we have an arrangement. I have my own place at Stinson Beach, and stay over at Carson's, that's his name, a couple of times a week.*"

"*Are you going to marry?*"

"*No. I don't think so.*"

"*Is he like me. No of course not! He could not be as handsome! You must send a photo.*"

At this point the ever-serious Benoît had interrupted Didi's non-stop flow of questions:

"You say your clinic is called Simone deB, and I assume you mean

Simone de Beauvoir. Do you want to be like her?"

"Well, if you mean divesting myself of bourgeois respectability, I'm not even close on that one. But as I told you a minute ago, I want to be the one who invents who I am."

Their conversation continued, alternating between Didi's somewhat outrageous questions and Benoît's serious efforts to get to know what Morgan was like, giving Morgan hope that that whatever reservations there may be, they were hitting it off so well that there would be more conversations. Thinking like a psychotherapist would during an initial session, she wanted there to be a next time.

She remembers them laughing at something Didi had just said when she heard a soft knock on her door, and then it opening just enough to let Pru push her face through the crack, raise her eyebrows and then quietly retreat, closing the door after her. Looking at her watch

Morgan realized her next patient was in the waiting room.

They agreed to *Skype* again in a week, with e-mails in between to set things up. As they were about to end, Benoît told her, This has gone very well. You have seduced us into liking you even though you may be an imposter. My lawyer told me that even if things seem very positive, we might still want something concrete. He had then mentioned a DNA test. Morgan had readily agreed; she had done the same procedure with Viktor.

It had ended with Didi suggesting they plan a meeting in New York, and Benoît giving him an Allard frown, making Didi stare into the camera and shrug his shoulders in a very French way.

Walking down the hall to the waiting room, Morgan thinks that the first thing she will tell Carson when they meet at Coles is, I met my brother today, and we talked.

Chapter Thirteen

Proxy

Something nags at him. Something is out of joint. Even with the meager information they have about Omar and Viktor, he thinks it is telling him something, and he is missing what it is. Usually, when he feels the tug, he passes it off as still being under siege mentality, but this time it does not reduce the tension and it keeps popping up, especially when he is with Morgan. Once again he blows it off.

Morgan sighs, and slips her arm through his, pulling him close. Their dinner was great, and with lots of talk, and the agreement that they would spend the coming weekend at her place at Stinson. Carson would come by himself on Saturday and leave Sunday evening rather than going over with her on Friday and staying through Monday. Still, Morgan was savoring it…he had not been there since she was hiding out from Wes Donovan.

"I'm liking this. César's was good, we finally have a weekend planned, and we're on our way to talk to Benoît and Didi."

"So. It's time for me to meet your family."

Finished with a late dinner at César's, they are heading back to Morgan's car and then to his place to wait until it is eight in the morning Paris time and *Skype* Benoît and Didi. This is to be Carson's debut conversation.

"It is. We have been talking more and more about you and planning a meeting in New York, so I thought it was time. I hope the four of us can come up with a window of opportunity for our meeting. Maybe we can get a mini vacation out of it."

"I hope I pass muster."

"I'm sure you will. Especially with Didi."

"What's that supposed to mean?"

"That you're cute."

Morgan's car is parked near Peet's at Walnut and Vine. She has traded her Lexus for a silver Audi A4 2.0T hatchback. It is another step in her post-Viktor era of change and re-invention: she has moved to Stinson, the studio on Tunnel is on the market. Soon she will be spending the weeknights in a condo in the city.

"Didi is a bit of a cannonball, but he's sweet and good for Benoît. I think Benoît would be depressed without him. Anyway, Didi is the one who keeps asking process questions. I think it makes Benoît nervous, but he goes along with it. I think talking about our motivations and feelings and our relationships has helped us to become close.

"But their lawyer, Vincent, is always in the background, and seems a combination of cautiousness and suspiciousness. One Vincent intervention is taking the DNA sample in New York. I had readily agreed to do it here, but I guess he, Vincent, wanted witnesses."

"So. You do it in New York."

"Right."

The phrase, *window of opportunity*-Morgan had used it earlier-flits through his mind, and he immediately knows the answer to the nagging puzzle about Omar and Viktor. Taking Morgan by the elbow, he hurries her toward her car.

"What?"

"Tell you when we're back at my place."

Then he slows. Ahead of them, a man gets out of his car, and, not bothering to lock it, walks in their direction. He is a white guy about the same height as Carson, black leather jacket over a black T-shirt, baggy jeans, and a black beanie pulled over his ears. He is in the process of swinging a backpack over his shoulders as he passes them without making eye contact.

Man, am I twitchy! "I think I'm a little jumpy."

Morgan is surprised and is about to reply, What ever for, when he says, "Shit."

Shocked, she watches Carson turn and charge toward the man who had just walked past them, but is now running toward them, tackling him and pushing him to the ground.

Morgan's first thought is to run, run to safety, but she will not leave Carson, standing rooted to the pavement, watching him grapple with the stranger.

Carson hears the running feet from behind.

It's the black beanie. "Shit." He turns and charges the assassin who is loping toward them, a hand holding his backpack by its handle, the other rummaging in one of its compartments. Startled to see his quarry attacking him he slows, becoming a better target. Carson crashes into him smashing his shoulder into the assassin's chest. The force of the tackle hurls them both to the sidewalk; Carson hears his assailant grunt as he lands on him. Tangled up with each other, they wrestle for control of the backpack while trying to break free of each other and regain their feet. They manage to get to their knees and Carson takes advantage of his balance and slugs him, hearing the crack of his fist against the other's cheek, missing his jaw. He takes another quick swing, hitting the assailant in the neck.

Coughing from the last blow he swings the backpack at Carson who falls back to avoid the blow which careens off the top of his head, and he falls backwards onto the sidewalk.

They both scramble to their feet. The backpack had sailed away when the guy swung at Carson, and he sees him holding a metal thermos, the kind that dermatologists use, struggling to unscrew the lock.

When Morgan sees the metal thermos, she knows what is going on. Viktor and Omar Rome have returned from the grave. They have sent their proxy to finish Donnie's job.

"Acid!" she screams.

Carson lands another blow, this time on target to the jaw, and sees the assassin's knee's buckle, and the swing of the thermos is slower giving him a chance to step back to avoid the blow. His foot slips off the curb, and he falls into the street.

There is a sudden lull in the combat as both men, Carson on his back, the assassin turning away from him, look in the direction of Morgan. Struggling to his feet, Carson sees her standing where he left her facing the man who wants to spray acid in her face. *Oh shit!*

Her assailant is startled, too and slows, staring at her standing in front of him, her outstretched arm pointing directly at him.

He throws his hands up in surrender. Frozen in place-for only a few clicks of the second hand although it seems forever to Morgan-they stare at each other before he turns and sprints away in retreat. Morgan lowers the pepper spray.

"Morgan. We must warn Benoît."

Morgan nods her head, but does not move. "Morgan. I'm afraid the same thing is going to happen to them."

"Damn that Viktor! It would be just like him to choreograph his revenge."

They rush to the car, and as Carson starts the engine, Morgan is already calling Benoît.

Chapter Fourteen

Carson Arrowsmith

Morgan

In his blue jeans and black T-shirt, Carson is in front of his Mac at the large wooden all-purpose table that both defines and commands the living space of his small studio. A half empty glass of *Louis Jadot Beaujolais*-on special at Safeway-sits beside the computer.

Carson glances at the menu bar of his Mac-a few minutes before one in the morning…it will be ten in the morning in Paris. After a frenetic week of phone calls and text messages, they had settled into using *FaceTime* three times a week-Tuesday, Thursday, and Sunday.

As they had feared there had been two attacks. Benoît and Didi had not escaped. On their way back to their apartment to talk to Morgan after a *petit déjeuner* at their favorite café, they were attacked, and a week passed before their lawyer, Vincent, had called with the news that their injuries were serious, but that they would survive. Less than twelve hours later Carson said goodbye to Morgan at SFO as she headed off to Paris.

Carson believes that Morgan's decision to go to her brother was the right one, and he supported it when she told him she was going. Before talking to him, she had discussed the possibility with Vincent who had readily agreed, she told him, that it was a good idea. He wishes she had discussed the possibility with him. With a protracted separation ahead of them, he wonders how this breakdown, or was it lack, of relational connection will play out between them during their time apart.

After another glance at the time, he opens *FaceTime*, highlighting Morgan's e-mail address and clicking on it, waiting for the computers to go through their connection process until a virtual Morgan, with headphones and microphone and white scarf in place, appears on his screen.

"Hi, Carson."

"Hey, Morgan. You look very fetching with that French combination of écharpe and écouteurs. You've gone Parisian in no time."

"The scarf is from the *Prix Unique, nine Euros,* near *Les Duex Magots*. Besides, I dress up for special occasions. And you know this girl goes for a guy in a black T-shirt."

"You getting on Ok?"

"Still in the thick of things… busy…."

"More comfortable in you digs?"

"A bit. Didi's place is very comfortable, but without the guys it's empty, and it gets lonely. Didi's parents will be here from Nice soon, and it will be better then.

"Their lawyer, Vincent and his wife, Jacqueline have been wonderful. They live in a fabulous place in Neuilly-there's even a hot tub under a glass roof just off the entry-and have invited me there, and have taken me to dinner at some very nice restaurants. Jacqueline and I have gone shopping several times. They wanted me to stay with them, but I wanted to be closer to Benoît."

"Speaking of the guys…how are they? Will they be home soon?"

"Daily progress. But, burns are hard to treat, and take time to heal. Benoît is quite depressed, and Didi is still in shock and also a lot of pain, and can't reach out. I think that even in the best of times Benoît needs Didi, and he's also feeling guilty-turns out Didi stepped in front of him and struggled with the creep with the acid, and his burns are more serious, especially his hands. They, Didi and the attacker, wrestled with the container…the guy ran away screaming when the acid got on his hands. I try to tell Benoît that because they fought back, it isn't as bad as it might be, but he's not listening to that a bit.

"Benoît also knows there will be scaring. He knows they won't be disfigured, but the scars will show. Also, Benoît and I both know that Viktor has taken his revenge. Regardless of who carries the scars, we are all scared."

"What about choice? You can say No to Viktor."

"Perhaps. But, the slope to your position is very steep."

Carson does not reply, and silence lingers between them.

"Anyway, as soon as I see Benoît's patients at the clinic in Belleville, I hurry back to the hospital, confer with their doctors, and sit with them. They aren't together, so I shuttle back and forth. But I need to hear about you…what are you up to?"

"Busy. Quite a few new patients, two new interns, interviewing two psychologists, one is a Buddhist monk. I think I'll have your caseload re-assigned by next week. I've sent the stuff on the list you sent me UPS. You should get it soon."

"Thanks. What are you doing for fun?"

"The usual; some hoops, handball, swimming…movies at PFA. I'm hanging out with Jon Cade. He has a new friend who has an online editing service, and we, Jon and I, are trying to figure out how to get involved. By the way Blanca called me wanting to have dinner. She said that since you deserted us we should get together and commiserate with each other."

"Blanca called you? You don't even know each other."

"I saw her only once at Whole Foods when you and I found each other. I put her off, said I'd call her in a week. I think she's a snitch, the one giving Gloria information about us."

"I wish you would hold off on that."

"Ok. I really didn't want to do it anyway."

"Has the SF police officer contacted you…Jessie Ritter?"

"Yes. She seemed, ah, different. What's it all about?"

"Different? I would say very interesting. She's the one who intervened when Wes was trying to drag Angela away from me. A couple of days ago she e-mailed me, wanting to talk. I told her I was in Paris and to get in touch with you."

"Well, we arranged to meet for coffee at Trieste on San Pablo."

Morgan picks up her computer, and, turning it away from her, pans the area, and Carson sees the familiar convergence of streets and the open market across the busy boulevard from where Morgan is sitting. It is where they stopped for a *Perrier* after meeting at Leda and Jon's place and before they went to his hotel.

"Look! Do you know where I am?"

"The café at Place Maubert."

"Yes! Do you remember the night we were here together?"

"I do. I remember everything. I miss you, Morgan."

"Ohhh…I miss you too. But…what's to be done? We haven't talked about when we're going to see each other again."

"I wish we had talked more before you left."

"We didn't talk much before I left, did we?"

"No. We didn't discuss your decision to leave."

"Are you mad?"

"A few ruffled feathers, but more questioning what it says about us as a couple."

A silence drifts between them-the two images stare at each other before Morgan breaks the silence.

"What does it say…about us?"

"Hard to say. Sign of the times? Even with smooth sailing, it's hard to find a balance between individuality and togetherness, especially when we're both in the habit of tilting toward individuality. I don't think we have to worry it. For now, though, with the uncertainty plus the distance we need to stay in touch."

"I'm not going to make excuses, but I think I should say sorry. I'm sorry I ruffled some of your feathers. Really."

"I accept and appreciate. Some of the feathers may be of the expectation kind so I must take responsibility for them."

"So…no long distance fighting?"

"No."

Again there is the trans Atlantic silence, this time acting as a punctuation allowing for the end of one line of discussion and as a bridge to another. He watches Morgan bite her lip and then take a breath.

"During our Skypes Benoît and Didi wanted to know about us. Like, do you have a boyfriend; do you live together…are you going to get married?"

"And…?"

"I told him you said we were a rockin and a rollin."

Carson laughs. "What did they do with that?"

"Comment? He said, What?

"So, behaving myself, I said I guess you could say we have an arrangement. I have my own place at Stinson Beach, and stay over at your place a couple of times a week. To the Are you going to get mar-

ried question I said, No I don't
think so.

"Thinking about it afterwards, I
felt a bit uneasy about using arrangement to describe us. But I did
say it so I had to assume there was
some truth to it. What I came to
was, OK, we have an arrangement now,
but it's moving toward something
that feels very good. Whatever that
something is, it will, if we want it
to, be more inclusive."

"Well, we can say what we want
as long as there is a rockin and a
rollin, though maybe we should keep
that between us."

"Ok, here we are like two bottles
of wine with a lot of promise, but
are going through the aging process.
When they're ready they should be
quite nice."

"Ok…very nice. Perhaps we should
consider two bottles of champagne
that are aging, but that need turn-

ing every now and then. A little attention is always very helpful."

"Oh yes! Bubbles. I like bubbles… a little attention now and then… waiting to pop our corks. Seriously though, we need to stay connected… well connected."

"And…I think…let each other in on our thoughts and feelings. Ok?"

"Ok. I'm still going to be lonely and miss you."

"Yes. No matter where I take my coffee in the morning, or in the evening fixing dinner or getting ready for bed, I'll be waiting for you."

Morgan looks at her image in the small window in the corner of her screen–she sees Benoît's spring at maximum look on her face and wills herself to relax. She is relieved that they are talking about them without going after each other…but feels stressed at the same time. She wants to be connected and share her thoughts and feelings. It just doesn't feel like a natural state, it's like she forgets and

has to be reminded. Right now, though….
Right now she is ready to be a bottle of
bubbly waiting to have her cork popped,
but not yet ready to be in love…certainly
not to say she is. *It's leading this way,
n'est pas*?

She watches Carson's image pull on his
ear, and then lean closer to the screen.

"I'm just guessing, but I bet you
could quite easily go native."

"Become a Parisian? Oh yes! If
you were here it would be very, very
easy. This is a wonderful place, so
cultured, so exciting. But, for now
I'm just an ex-pat."

Both are silent, as their im- ages
speed across a continent and an ocean to
each other's screens, and they contemplate the slow but steady, not always obvious, life of their relationship.

"Yes, an ex-pat on a mission.
Speaking of which, do you see an end
in sight?"

"I want to meet Didi's parents. I
think they support his relation- ship

with Benoît, but I want to see for myself. DiDi wants to go to Nice when they are out of the hospital. Can you come here?"

"I can't see that happening for a while. It's mostly being sure Café Simone deB is running smoothly. I hate to leave new patients so soon."

"Not even a long weekend?"

"That's what I am thinking. And believe me, as soon as possible."

"Well hurry. It's been too long."

"I'm definitely ready to carouse."

"Definitely. That's why I will be in my bedroom for our next FaceTime session."

"I'll be there…virtually, anyway. By the way, why not bring the guys here? It might really do them good to get away. We could all hang out. it would be a fresh start."

"I had thought of that. I would like it. It just doesn't seem like the right time to bring it up."

Carson sees Morgan glance at her watch and then sigh.

"Got to go. I always feel so much better after talking to you. Lonely, but feeling better."

"This is going to get me through the next couple of days."

Gloria

We are more resilient than we give ourselves credit for, and life is a naturally carrying forward process, we just don't know where it's taking us.

Carson pours more wine in his glass, then stares at it before pouring it back into the bottle, corking it, and going into the bathroom and washing his teeth. He moves the screen from between the table and the bed to in front of the side window, and retrieves his pajamas from under his pillow.

Headlights flash briefly against the closed shade sending shards of light through the slits; someone, he assumes, is using his driveway to back-up and change directions.

I hate that.

He is startled when there is a loud, urgent knocking at the front door. Peeking through the shades he sees a car in the driveway. The knocking continues as he goes to the door, peering through the small glass window with beveled edges. It is Gloria Belknap. He opens the door and she bursts in.

There is a look of madness about her; her hair is disheveled, the usual careful make-up is missing. The buttons are crooked on her white shirt—she is not wearing a bra—and it looks as if she quickly pulled on a pair of gray sweats and a pair flip-flops before she hurried from wherever she was. She is clutching one of her fancy purses with both hands.

Eyes wild and searching she stops a few feet from Carson who has retreated from her invasion. Suddenly her face softens, her lips quiver. Carson is surprised to see what seems to him a soft beauty radiating from her. In a small, placating voice, hardly audible, she says, "Help."

Just as suddenly the madness returns, and she screeches, "Where is she? Where's your bitch?"

"What can I do to help, Gloria."

She sways, blinking rapidly, and Carson thinks that for an instant vulnerability fueled by pain slipped by the rage, but her demons quickly reasserted their control.

"Where is she?"

"She's not here."

"Where?"

"She's gone to Paris."

Gloria looks triumphant. "She's left you. I knew she would. You deserve it. Now you've lost both of us."

"Let me help."

"You pig! Don't you patronize me!"

Carson's breath catches in his throat as he watches Gloria pull a small caliber automatic from her purse, pointing it at his face. It fits perfectly in her hand, the whiteness of her skin contrasting with the burnished blueness of the weapon-softness and hardness...madness and death.

"That chair." Using the gun as a pointer she directs Carson to move a chair away from the table and place it in the center of the room.

"Sit." She leans against the edge of the table, the gun still pointed at him.

"Frightened? Are you scared?"

"Yes."

"Ha! Little man. Maybe you're going to piss in your pants. Maybe I won't shoot you if you piss in your pants."

Carson is sure that very soon Gloria is going to shoot him between the eyes. For some reason the thought calms him; his only concern is that the small caliber bullet is powerful enough to kill him, not leave him a vegetable. He watches Gloria. At first she seemed mad, in a psychotic state, but with enough semblance of reality left to ask for help. But since pulling the gun from her purse her mood has changed. Now she is taunting him after setting the stage, and it seems she is now playing out something she has rehearsed, perhaps an obsessive fantasy.

"You've been thinking about doing this for a long time, haven't you?" It is hard for him to keep his voice from cracking.

"Your squaw is a thief."

"We fell for each other before we knew anything about you. We met in Paris…we fell in love with each other in Paris."

"Did you fuck her in Paris?"

"We became lovers in Paris. We have not stolen from you." Gloria no longer seems crazy…on autopilot, perhaps, but not crazy. *How long do I have*? *H'mm*. *Stolen*?

"I want you to be happy. Morgan and I don't want to make you unhappy."

"I was rejected by BAKS." She sounds like the old Gloria.

"Morgan did not participate in the selection. She did not vote."

Gloria's arm waivers, is he getting though to her?

"We all have lists of people who have hurt us. But, please believe me, you're not on my list, and neither Morgan nor I have done anything to be on yours."

"Being a single woman, living alone; it's not easy. And, being a professional woman doesn't make it any easier. When we talked the first time you called you sounded so nice and so interesting that I was optimistic for the first time in a very long time.

"Then, when we hit it off at our first meeting I thought, this is perfect. Even when you turned down my dinner invitation it didn't bother me. Give him time I said. I know he likes me. Then. Then…. What went wrong Carson? What did I do wrong? Why did you turn your back on me?"

"You didn't do anything wrong, Gloria."

"Then why?"

"I was glad to meet you, I looked forward to using your office. But that was all. I had met Morgan in Paris, I was hoping to reunite with her here in the Bay Area."

"But you met me!"

"I did, that's true. But to be honest, I wasn't looking for a relationship."

"You must have known how I felt about you."

"Not really."

"How could you, knowing how I felt about you, stand me up like you did? We had made a date you know."

"I screwed up. I had just reunited with Morgan, and it completely slipped my mind. I told you then that I was sorry, and I still am."

The madness returns; Gloria shakes the gun at him. "How could you like her better than me? I have so much more to offer you than she will ever have."

"I'm not trying to make you mad, but I don't have the feelings toward you that you think I do. It's not anything that you did. I just don't have the strong feelings toward you that you wish I do."

"So, I'm supposed to believe your squaw didn't have anything to do with this."

"She did not steal me from you."

"You made me grovel. You made me vulnerable. I had to plead; I had to open myself to you while you stood there, silent and withholding. Then you said, No. Do you remember what I said before you sent me away?"

"Yes, I do."

Gloria takes a step back, keeping her eyes on him, the gun aimed at his forehead. She pulls on the cord of her sweats, pulling until it is pulled free. The sweats fall to the floor. Next the shirt falls to the floor.

"Do you want me?"

I'm dead. Carson knows what his last words have to be.

Time to move this along. Rising slowly he faces Gloria-the gun aimed at his face rises along with him. He wonders if he will see the flash, or hear the shot. Will it hurt?

Silent, Gloria watches him.

"I love Morgan."

The silence remains between them. Gloria offers no response…she continues to stare at him over the barrel of the gun.

"Gloria, please. Please put the gun down…get dressed and go home."

Gloria sighs. "I'm sorry." Staring at him, she puts the gun to her temple and pulls the trigger.

Silence. Gloria and Carson stare at each other.

Safety is on!

Lunging at Gloria and crashing into her, he struggles to grab the gun, and when he gets a grip on her wrist he shakes it until the gun flies across the room. Scrambling to his feet he hurries to retrieve it, stopping when he hears Gloria screaming as she opens the front door.

He catches the naked and screaming Gloria halfway down the driveway, and after getting both arms around her from the back, hefts her back inside, kicking the door shut behind him. Gloria has collapsed or lost consciousness…she is limp in his arms. He lets go of her, letting her drop onto the sofa. She is pale, her eyes half open, sweat covers her body. Checking, he finds her pulse rapid and strong. There is a metallic odor to her breath. Grabbing a blanket from the bed he wraps it around her, and she moans as he tucks it around her. Carson reasons that there is the possibility that she has either stopped taking some kind of medication or has overdosed.

"Gloria. You're safe. No more being stolen from…. Have you taken anything…a lot of anything?"

She moans, but says nothing.

He picks up the phone and dials 9-1-1. He hears sirens; someone heard her screams…the police are on the way. His forehead itches, and he scratches it while he reports the emergency and his address.

Gloria moans and then sighs, struggling under the blanket. "Help me."

Checking Gloria he finds her pulse and heartbeat rapid but not overly so; her pale skin is no longer clammy. After removing the clip, Carson puts it in his pocket and the gun on the table, and, retrieving his wine glass and the bottle from the kitchen, pours himself some Beaujolais. Stepping around Gloria's clothes, he pulls the chair back to the table and sits down to wait.

Acknowledgements

Marcia Dyer-Crapo, my wife-I hope Carson and Morgan discover what we have.

Laura Sample Mattos, editor-she helped me focus on what I wanted to say.

Editor Mike Valentino-Mike...who made my words bright and clear on every page.

John Mattos, illustrator-he designed the cover that makes you want to pick up my book and see what's inside.

Debra Layton and Sue Bender-each with their own style, they offered sage and informed advise.

Thanks to the following who gave their time so readily, and their comments so willingly-Dane and Jay Christensen, Mike and Jayne Whichello, Celeste Crapo Howell, Joe and Lynne Halperin, and Mona Pang. There are many others too, friends and marriage and family therapy graduate students who listened and shared their thoughts and feelings. Thanks.

About the Author

Steve Crapo is a psychologist and Professor Emeritus at California State University, East Bay. He was a teacher at Castlemont High School in Oakland and a counselor at Abbott Middle School in San Mateo before joining the faculty at Cal State. His practice of psychotherapy included individuals, couples and families.

He is a native of San Francisco, and lives with his wife Marcia in Berkeley.

Made in the USA
Lexington, KY
10 September 2012